GOD D... ...
ZOMBIE
CHAINSAW
MURDERER

SEAN MALIA THOMPSON

A NICTITATING BOOKS PUBLICATION

Also from Nictitating Books:

Screaming Creatures

Astrum

House of Blood and Teeth

We Are Here to Hurt Each Other

God Damn Zombie Chainsaw Murderer
by Sean Malia Thompson
Proofread by Tiffany Morris
Published by Nictitating Books

Cover and Layout by Yves Tourigny
Interior Formatting by Michael Adams

Custom fonts used in this book:
Foul Fiend by Sinister Fonts
https://www.1001fonts.com/users/savage/

CONTENT WARNING

THE FOLLOWING BOOK CONTAINS:

-EXTREME, GRAPHIC VIOLENCE

-HARD DRUG USE

-SEXUAL ASSAULT

-SUICIDE

For my sister Gillian, who sat with me in the living room watching most of the slashers that inspired this novel.

(Yo, this shit is fucking insane Gill, lol.)

"Pick a song and sing a yellow nectarine
Take a bath I'll drink the water that you leave
If you should die before me ask if you could bring a
friend
Pick a flower hold your breath and drift away"
-Stone Temple Pilots

"Shame shame
Throw yourself away
Give me little bits of
More than I can take
If it sits upon your tongue
Or naked in your eyes
Give me little bits of
More than I can try

Throw yourself away
Throw yourself away"
-Soundgarden

They arrive at the old Shell station at 2 PM, on Friday July 15th, 1996. Melanie is the type of tired one can only be after a long car ride. The day is blisteringly hot, a humidity to make her t-shirt stick to her skin from sweat. Her auburn hair is plastered to her lightly freckled forehead.

They are all pleasantly surprised to see the place. Jake, who drove, suggested they get last minute supplies at the store attached to the gas station. Melanie knew he just wanted another pack of Marlboro Reds. Melanie has been dating Jake for just over 6 years at this point, and she knows that when he drinks, as they all plan to over the course of the weekend, he smokes like a fucking chimney. Jake is in decent shape, his time in the military showing in his arms, shoulders, and chest through his Alice in Chains shirt. His hair is light brown, a bit shaggy with bangs also sticking to his forehead from the heat.

"Hey, try not to jack off in the bathroom," Amy says to David, who smiles a snaggle-toothed grin before replying "I make no promises."

"Creep," Jake mumbles under his breath.

"You going in?" Melanie asks Jake, who shrugs and follows them inside.

The store is cool, cold, with tiny white metal shelves and an old air conditioning unit that sounds like it's about to blast off into space. The man behind the register has a long white beard that matches his long white hair. He's chewing tobacco, and has a small plastic cup full of his used chew in front of him on the register that resembles raw sewage. Melanie almost dry heaves. The charm of the locals, she supposes.

"You ain't from around here," the old man says, staring straight at Melanie. He hacks a glob of spit into the cup.

"What gave it away, the fact we have all our teeth?" David says. Amy elbows him lightly in the ribs.

"Your car has Massachusetts plates, smart aleck," the old man says, punctuating his statement with another large glob of tobacco spit into the cup.

"I'm just kidding, old timer. Don't have a cow, man."

"Really, dude?" Jake mutters, rolling his eyes.

"You all headed out to the woods to do that liberal disaffected youth sex partying?"

"Uh… maaaaybe?" Melanie says, eyeing Jake. Jake just sighs and walks up to the counter.

"Well not that anyone ever listens, but them woods is dangerous. Had a friend's cousin go missing in them woods."

"Pack of Marlboro Reds," Jake says. The old cashier rings him up, taking his money and giving him change, frowning at him all the while.

"Those things'll kill ya," the old man says, hocking up more spent chew.

"Much obliged," Jake says, pocketing the pack of cigarettes and telling Melanie, "see you in the car."

Melanie steps closer to the old man, and asks "what did you mean about the woods being dangerous. Like, bears?"

"Oh, only beast you got to worry about ain't no bear."

"Then what?"

Melanie leans in, the old man motioning for her to get closer. The old man whispers to her.

"God damn zombie chainsaw murderer."

"What was that dude's damage?" Jake asks the group at large.

"Heavy inbreeding?" Amy says, brushing her bleachy blonde hair out of her face.

They all burst into laughter, David especially, who cracks a shit-eating grin.

"What the fuck ever, let's go have some fun," David says, cracking open a beer in the back of the sedan.

"Damn Dave, can you chill, for like, one fucking second?" Jake asks.

"You chill, I'm here to par-tay."

"Please don't say it like that," Jake says.

"What? Like paaaaar-taaaaaaaay?"

"God I fucking hate you," Jake says, sighing.

"We all hate him," Amy says, leaning in and planting a wet kiss on David, who giggles like a moron.

"How much farther?" Melanie says.

"I don't know, about thirty minutes?" Jake answers, hands resting on the steering wheel. The green Toyota Camry continues its smooth traversal of the tree-surrounded road.

"And you called the guy at the canoe place?" David asks from the back seat, then drinks from his can of beer.

"Yup. Fairly sure I called the guy."

"Fairly sure?"

"Who can tell with this shit. We should be fine, though. Things are all set up."

They drive in silence for a time. Melanie stares at the tree cover as the vehicle travels; the verdant foliage, and heavy canopies like standing sentinels of nature. The rest are having a conversation, but the words all fall away to her. To Melanie, all is the natural landscape. Until Jake speaks her name.

"I'm sorry, what did you ask me?"

"When's the last time you went camping?"

"Oh. Um… jeez, let's see. It was many, many years ago."

"Where abouts?"

"Oh, just New Hampshire. Only a day."

"Well, Lake George camping is going to be intense. The lake is beautiful, and we get this whole island to ourselves. It'll be an experience like no other."

Melanie smiles. Jake smiles back. She always did love that smile.

"So we're canoeing in?" she asks.

"Yeah," Jake says.

"How big is the island?"

"Oh, pretty damn big. A few miles," Jake says.

"That's really rad," Melanie says. She wicks the sweat from her forehead with the sleeve of her Hole t-shirt.

"Isn't it, though?" Jake says.

"Hey, anyone want to smoke a doob?" David blurts out. He's the only one of them without longer hair, his short-cropped dark black hair making Melanie so jealous in this heat. She wishes she had a shaved head in heat like this; just go full Sinead O'Connor.

"Fuck dude, can you wait until we get to the island?" Jake says, a biting anger in his voice.

"Oh come on, Davey want smokey."

"Would you be offended if I killed your boyfriend?" Melanie asks Amy, who just shrugs.

"Go nuts, he's just dead weight."

"I'm your dead weight," David says, kissing Amy on the cheek, who giggles, and lightly pushes him off of her. Melanie rolls her eyes, she can't help herself.

"Okay, here we are, I guess," Jake says.

Jake parks in a dirt lot by the canoe rental shop. A small wooden shack in front of the racks of rental boats has, in white letters on a wooden sign at the top, "We All Float Over Here." A man in a very floppy beige bucket hat, with neon pink swim trunks and Teva flip flops waves to them, zinc prominently slathered on his nose.

"Well howdy there folks!"

"Oh lord…" Melanie mumbles under her breath.

"What was that, Miss?"

"I said hello!" Melanie says, overcorrecting in a very obvious way the canoe rental guy doesn't seem to notice at all.

"You the nice folks who called about renting two canoes?"

"Yes sir!" David says, slapping the man on the back, whose smile lights up even brighter.

Again, Melanie rolls her eyes. She wishes she was less cynical, but this is the 90s, so over it is totally the style, plus, it's just, like, her personality. Melanie has always been like this, ever since she was a little girl. Amy jokes that she's like if Daria was hot, and admittedly, Melanie has never known the correct response to this sentiment. She's always got vibes from Amy, though—vibes she doesn't entirely mind. They are, however, vibes she suspects David will likely not be very thrilled with.

There was that party she went to on Halloween of 1995, the one where Melanie went as the Bride of Frankenstein, and Amy went as the bee girl from the Blind Melon video. Amy got incredibly wasted and started making out with her. Such a thrilling turn of events Melanie could never have even dreamed of, like someone reached into her head and pulled a fantasy directly out, made it tangible, and touchable. Melanie expected if anything like that ever happened to her, maybe she would be scared, or maybe grossed out, but nothing could be further from the truth. It was like a switch had flipped inside of her, arguably a switch that was always very close to flipping no matter what. For those brief moments Melanie was in heaven, a transcendent experience she had yet to match. Thankfully, David was probably even more wasted than they were, and never noticed. Jake had maybe been at the party? Melanie has trouble remembering.

"Melanie?"

"I'm sorry, what was that?"

"We're going to start unloading the car, come on," Jake says.

This is what they do, Melanie making sure she has her back up flannel and a back up pair of Airwalks, while David of course makes sure the beer and weed is on board. Jake is in charge of food, and Amy is in charge of firewood, though come to that Melanie suspects they can use the axe they're bringing to chop some wood, and there's bound to be sticks and stuff. The day goes from slightly cloudy to outright rainy fairly quickly, like God heard their plan to canoe across a body of water with supplies and thought "as if."

The lake is beautiful. Jake was right about that. Cool blue water surrounded by vast wilderness on all sides. A pristine landscape as far as the eye can see. A lot of speedboats, which very quickly makes her realize why this lake is so choppy; why there are 3 foot waves crashing on the surface of the water. Rain begins belting down from the heavens like angry little droplets, that would soak through her neon t-shirts, flannels, and jeans with ripped knees except they all have waterproof bags.

Jake leads the charge in the first canoe with her, Amy, and David pushing them from the shore. The boat rental guy helps David and Amy into their canoe. Melanie can just barely see this through the storm.

The going is hard, waves crashing into the boats launching them into the air, Melanie straining with her arm muscles to hold onto the paddle with all her might through the choppy water. She fears the canoe might topple over, but Melanie in particular has wrapped her clothing and various other items in individual plastic bags; she can be somewhat neurotic. Always seemed to her it was better to be safe than sorry, as humdrum as this sounded. And praise Alanis, Melanie is happy she went all out in rain and waves like this.

The journey feels epic in scope, like she's in some adventure film; water splashing over the side of the canoe into her face, rain pelting down, wind howling. She isn't thrilled with being absolutely soaked, but she's just spotted the island, a haven of possible dryness.

"That's the island ahead!" Jake shouts over the storm.

"Woo!" she shouts back.

She hears Jake laughing over the storm. Melanie loves it when Jake smiles, when he laughs. He so rarely seems happy, nowadays. She pushes these thoughts out of her mind.

The shore to the island is now less than a mile, Melanie thinks so, at least. Gauging distance is hard on the water. Especially in a storm like this. She isn't sure how long the journey was supposed to be, but it has felt like the better part of an hour getting to the island.

"Well, there it is," Jake says, loudly.

"Was that a Jurassic Park reference?"

"I… maybe?" he replies, also loudly.

The shore approaches and Melanie feels the canoe hit land, and jostle her and Jake. She clambers out of the canoe, nearly tipping the boat as her shoes slide in the wet sand.

"Are we supposed to come in like that?" she shouts over the storm.

"Uh, babe, that's why we're using a rental," Jake shouts back.

"Whatever," she shouts.

"Killer," he shouts back.

"Let's just unload the fucking canoes and get up a tarp already!" she shouts. She's real sick of fucking shouting.

Jake gives her the thumbs up. They unload supplies, stacking them beneath a large oak tree to shield them from the rain. Melanie has plenty of dry clothes, so she also helps Amy and David as they pull up on shore. She helps lug the firewood with David; she puts the logs under a flannel from her bag. Amy brings up the rest of her gear, and David slaps himself in the head. "Dur! We need to drag the boats onto shore!" He runs back in the direction of the canoes.

The rest go back to help David. After all, he shouldn't have to do it all by himself. David and Amy drag the one canoe, Melanie and Jake get the other. The work is slow, dragging the canoes through the wet sand. Still, they manage. For good measure Jake takes two pieces of rope and ties each piece around a pine tree, the other end of the rope around the metal loop on the bow of each canoe.

"So where do we want to camp?" David asks, scratching his butt through his acid wash jeans.

"Let's aim for somewhere a little farther away from the shoreline," Amy says. "I don't want to wake up all wet."

"That makes one of us…" Melanie mutters.

"What was that?" Amy says.

"Nothing!" Melanie shouts back.

"I'm not that far away, Mel, you don't need to shout."

"The wind was…"

Melanie finally notices the wind has died down now that they are among the trees.

"Ah. Nevermind."

The walk under the canopy of pines and oaks lends the journey a mythical feeling, this is how it seems to Melanie. Something out of one of those dorky fantasy novels Jake likes to read sometimes, the type that usually have a dragon on the cover. The rain still splashes down, soaking her through (she's only wearing a flannel, and not even a heavy one at that) and she's quick to notice the others look equally miserable, especially Jake who lugs firewood, face grimacing with the strain. Melanie likes seeing him like this —not in pain, but using his muscles, sweating in the forest.

This is honestly a nice change of pace from their usual life together. Cohabitating at the apartment in Framingham. The cruddy little apartment next to the adult video store. Say what you will about perverts, but they're great at creating affordable housing.

Jake has been in a funk for months now. He's irritable, and when he isn't angry he seems to be sort of vaguely sad. Melanie has tried all she can to help him, to soothe him. But she's not a mental health professional. Their life together has become like some sort of indie drama, except there's no pithy dialogue, or grand romantic gestures, or real excitement. Things are just sort of sad, sort of boring, sort of not the life she had wanted for herself.

They find a nice spot with a tiny bit of tree cover, an opening in the middle so it's safe to have the firepit. Melanie is absolutely exhausted, *need to sit my ass down*, she thinks. Melanie drops her gear off with a huff. Jake gives her a wink as he drops his own stuff to the ground, pine needles and mud spraying as he drops his waterproof bag. Amy and David are making out in the corner. David feels up Amy's ass; he's really going for it, squeezing her butt cheeks hard.

Melanie both sighs and inwardly shudders. She wishes those were her hands on her friend's legs, feeling the warm flesh underneath her jeans, feeling the heat of her deep inside.

"Hey, Melanie, help me with the tarp," Jake says, from behind her.

"Yeah. Yeah, sure."

They stretch the tarp between two pine trees, placing the fire wood and the cooler of food underneath. Jake kisses her on the mouth, and she reciprocates, but keeps one eye on David and Amy as she does.

"Who's hungry?" David says, giving Amy one last slap on the ass for good measure.

"Hell yeah, what's on the menu?" Melanie says. She does finally find a log to sit on: screw the rain, she's already sorta soaked, anyway.

"Well, since it's probably going to take a while to get the fire going—"

"I assume it'll take a while," Jake says, placing small twigs in a pile of crumpled newspaper, frowning all the while.

"Right, so like, unless for whatever reason it's easier with this stuff, let's eat something prepackaged."

"Such as?" Amy asks, brushing her bright blonde hair from her wet face.

"Pop Tarts anyone?" David asks. "What the hell," Melanie says. She looks over to Amy who is staring at

David. Melanie can't read Amy's expression. Perhaps her friend is a little angry?

They rip into the cinnamon Pop Tarts as the storm rages on, Jake having volunteered to try to get the fire going. He swears under his breath, trying to get the fatwood going as the rain falls like the tears of chubby angels on a diet. David goes over to help him, trying to block the rain with his body, trying to block the wind.

This leaves Amy sitting beside Melanie, on folding chairs they've brought. Amy with her soft lips, and warm blue eyes. Amy with her blonde hair, and her energy; a lightness to her friend's vibe, a peaceful playfulness Melanie has never quite gotten over. Amy is speaking but Melanie can't hear what she's saying, transfixed as she is with Amy's mouth, her lips, her eyes; it's impossible for Melanie to take in what her friend is actually conveying.

"What's that darling?"

"Darling?"

"Um, sorry, I mean, you know, what's up girlfriend?"

"Oh, much better, you weirdo."

Amy gives her a playful little punch in the ribs.

"Sorry."

"I'm just fucking with you, Melanie!"

I wish you would, Melanie thinks.

"I was saying do you like shrooms?"

"Um… what?"

"You know, magic mushrooms!"

"Um…"

"Oh come on! Don't look at me like that!"

"Like what, you brought hallucinogens? Like, are you going to do them?"

"No, I'm going to juggle them. Yes, I plan to take them. Everyone is."

"Everyone?"

"Yeah. Jake, and, David and me."

"So I'm the only one who didn't know about this?"

"Oh, come on sweetie, we didn't want to freak you out."

"Oh yeah, so springing the drugs on me last minute was a thoughtful gesture?"

"Aw, damn it Melanie, don't be like this!"

"Be like what?"

"Like this! The party pooper! The stick in the mud!"

"I am not a stick in the mud!"

Melanie looks over to Jake for reassurance. Jake simply shrugs.

"Oh, well thank you for that bode of confidence."

"It's vote of confidence."

"What did I say?"

"Bo—"

"Look whatever, just, like, just don't take them without telling me, okay! I'll fucking do it, just… don't exclude me. I don't want to be the only one of you not tripping."

"Have you ever done them?"

"I mean, no."

"You'll be fine. We can give you a smaller amount."

She tries her best not to let the unease show on herself, and has no idea if she succeeds.

"What are they like?"

"You smoke weed, right?"

"Sometimes."

"It's sort of like weed but stronger. And more floaty."

Amy makes a blissed out face, exaggeratedly content, letting her hands gently sway above her.

"Will I have a nightmare freakout?"

"Oh honey, no, no no. You'll be fine! We're all here, and we're all your friends! Nothing but good vibes!" Amy gives her a hug. Melanie tries not to let her eyes roll back in her head like a dog having its back scratched.

"What, did you find that on a t-shirt somewhere? 'Nothing but Good Vibes,' and then the back says like some resort name or some shit."

"Hey babe, David and I are gonna go on a walk," Jake says, giving her a look like *what is up with you?*

"What?" Melanie asks, she isn't sure why she asks, she heard him the first time, her brain is just being funny today.

"We're going for a walk," Jake says, flatly.

"Sure thing," Melanie says. She watches Jake and David wander off, then disappear at the treeline.

She is sizing Amy up, feeling a shiver work its way down her spine. Melanie hopes Amy can't hear her gulping down the rush of saliva to her mouth. Melanie hopes Amy doesn't notice a lot of things. And, simultaneously, and paradoxically, she wishes her friend would notice a lot.

She wishes Amy would notice absolutely everything.

David hits the joint, cupping his hand over the end to keep the thing from going out in the rain.

"You know, Melanie is pretty hot."

"Oh, I remember,' Jake says, taking the joint from David, taking his own puff. He wears a green Starter rain jacket with the Boston Celtics logo on the back.

"You're a lucky man," David says, giving him a light punch on the arm.

"Hey, Amy's nothing to sneeze at," Jake says, taking a final pull off the joint, and squeezing his thumb and index finger over the cherry to put it out, placing the roach in his jacket pocket.

"God, can you believe all of this?" David says, gesturing with his arms outstretched, spinning in a circle. "This is wild! Absolutely nuts."

"I know, right? All of this is so crazy."

And it really was, Jake was so glad they'd come here. It took a lot of doing but now that they were here he felt great. A little apprehensive, maybe, but great.

"Ah, to be young and alive," David says.

"Fuckin' A, brother," Jake says.

"You think you're gonna get lucky this weekend?"

"Dude…"

"What? I know you're thinking it."

"I don't know, most likely," Jake says.

"Oh, come on man, this is a once in a lifetime opportunity! You gotta get that dick wet!"

David whacks Jake in the crotch, who coughs and wobbles a bit.

"Fuck man, that hurt."

"Aw shit, sorry dude. Don't know my own strength I guess."

"Well don't hit me in the dick again, ay?"

"Okay, I'll do my best." David says, staring off into the sky. "I ever tell you I saw a UFO?"

"Great segue,"Jake says, face still scrunched up in mild discomfort.

Being friends with David can be a chore sometimes. He's constantly fucking with people. They've known each other since the 6th grade, when Mrs. Borges yelled at David for sticking a pencil up his nose, for cracking jokes in class, for existing (frankly, Jake can more than understand). And Jake doesn't know what it says about him but they became fast friends. So, over the years Jake has learned to take everything David says with a hefty grain of salt. A fast food level of salt. A whole ocean's worth of damn salt.

"I'm not kidding," David says.

"Sure you're not. Stop messing with me, man."

"I'm fucking serious, dude. I was driving on 95 at like 2 in the morning."

"Wait, wait, wait."

Jake places his hand on David's shoulder, to stare directly into his red eyes.

"You are telling me you saw a UFO over one of the busiest highways in Massachusetts?"

"Yeah, dude!"

"Oh fuck off, I cry bullshit."

"I swear to you it's the truth," David says, a hurt look on is face.

"Well, go ahead and tell me your obviously bullshitty story, you absolute pants-on-fire liar."

"So, I was driving on 95, and I was sort of hungover."

This news somehow does not shock Jake. David drank a whole lot, most of the time.

"Where were you drinking?"

"Does it matter?"

"I mean, no, I'm just wondering."

"Alison's house."

"How long ago was this?"

"Last year."

"Oh man, you need to stop doing that shit. Amy is going to fucking kill you."

David could never keep his dick in his pants. This was something Jake had known about David for many years. This didn't used to bother Jake as much, but then David started dating Amy, their mutual friend, and suddenly his serial philandering pissed him off. It pissed him off a whole lot.

"Look, that's my fucking business, so like, let me just get back to the UFO story."

"Fine, fine. Lay on, Macduff."

"I'm driving on 95, with this killer headache. And it's like two in the afternoon. I look over off the highway, just, you know, there's not a ton of traffic. And then I see it. This shiny metal craft, traveling at speed towards the ground. At what looked like a forty-five degree angle."

"What did it look like?"

Jake is starting to wonder if David is actually full of shit. He doesn't have his typical shit-eating grin.

"It looked like one of those single passenger planes. But entirely silver."

"Dude, an airplane? Really?"

"What? It was an unidentified flying object. That is the very definition of what the damn thing is."

"Okay, so… what happened?"

David screws up his face in a way that makes Jake just want to walk away. For a person he supposedly is good friends with, he definitely hates the shit out of David, like, often.

"Well, the thing suddenly looked like it caught on fire."

"What?"

"Dude, yeah. It was nuts. This single passenger plane-looking-thing catches on fire, and lands off in the woods off 95. I'm expecting an explosion, right? But there's nothing. I checked the news later. Also nothing."

"Do you think you hallucinated it?"

"I mean, maybe? But why would it be a plane then? Wouldn't I have hallucinated a traditional looking UFO?"

"That's true."

David looks at the surrounding wilderness. The stress seems to melt off his face.

"God, it's pretty out here."

"Heck yeah, dude."

Jake loves the wilderness. Being in nature really helps with all the intrusive thoughts.

"Come on, let's head back before I'm soaked through," David says, turning and walking away.

Jake follows close behind as they wander back to camp. He lets the cool air enter his lungs, holds it inside like a secret. He wants to keep this place with him long after they leave.

Amy drinks a beer, glad the rain has finally let up. She's changed into a new pair of jean shorts, the one's frayed at the bottom where the ends rest along her inner thighs, and lower butt. She knows David goes crazy when she wears these shorts, and the choice is intentional. Amy wants him to notice her, to really appear to appreciate her. He so rarely lately seems to care about her in any way.

She's had a feeling for some time now that David has been sleeping around. There were subtle things, at first. David saying he needed to stay late at the office. Last minute "drinks with the guys." But soon enough things became less subtle. Everything became downright obvious. Long hairs on his coats that were decidedly not her own. Condoms in his wallet when she was on birth control. Getting phone calls he'd take into the other room, speaking in a hushed tone; this was probably the most obvious, as David had never been a quiet person, basically ever.

She wonders where she went wrong, sometimes. Amy would stare at the ceiling, sleepless, wondering just what it is about her that can't keep David around. She knows she's cute, she's had plenty of people swoon over her. So what is it that keeps David from staying? Is it even her fault?

She hears a rustling in the bushes behind her.

"What was that?"

Jake turns to her, his own beer in his hand raised halfway to his mouth. "What was what?"

"I thought I heard something in the bushes behind me."

David looks, squinting.

"Hey! Monster! Come on out!"

"David!"

"What, I'm just fucking around," David says, then belches, loudly.

"What if it's a bear?"

David laughs. "Then we're fucked, and that's that," he says, finishing off his beer and tossing the empty over his shoulder.

"How can you be so calm?" Amy asks him. David frowns at her. She really hates him sometimes. Amy wonders why she's still even with the bastard. She suspects a lot of the group feel a similar way, perhaps in slightly different variations.

"Oh, what, it's not a bear," David says.

"And how do you know that?" Amy says.

"Because it would, like, make bear noises."

"What like 'Hey Boo-Boo, let's get some pic-a-nic baskets?'" Jake asks.

"Eat an entire bag of dicks," David says, flipping Jake the bird.

"It could easily be a bear, David," Amy says.

"Oh stop, you're just being fucking overly dramatic, *as always.*"

"Well I hope that fucking bear rips your dick off!" Amy says, huffing off to the cooler to grab another beer.

"Trouble in paradise…" Jake mutters over to Melanie. And Melanie can't help herself, she perks up, because maybe her dreams aren't so foolish after all. Maybe Amy and her might have the opportunity on this trip to really connect. Physically, and spiritually.

Melanie is in love with Amy. This terrifies her, but there is no denying the truth anymore, not to herself, anyway. And this weekend is as good a time as any to make a confession.

Night has fallen in earnest when they finally get the fire going, with a good coal bed roaring. They roast hot dogs over the open flame. Jake's happy, since he's fucking starving. All of them are absolutely ravenous.

"Yay, pig anuses!" Amy cries, then bursts out laughing. Amy is now quite drunk, as Jake can tell. He might not know much in this life but he knows a drunk. Lord knows he is one…

"Think fast, dipshit," David says, handing him a hot dog in a bun, slathered in mustard and relish.

"No ketchup?" Jake asks.

"An inferior condiment," David replies, taking a bite of his own dog.

"Dumbass," Jake mutters to himself.

Jake has noticed a rift in the relationship between Amy and David, perhaps before any of the rest. He did sleep with Amy a few weeks ago. He doesn't think Melanie knows yet, and he's not exactly proud of what he did. All the same, he enjoyed himself.

He was surprised when Amy called and asked him to come over; figured she would ask him about David, and the plethora of women he'd fucked. He was gearing up to finally nail the bastard and of course David deserved it—just because the dude was his friend didn't mean he wasn't an enormous, cheating asshole.

Of course, he'd got in the door and Amy had proceeded to kiss him, to push him against the wall and demand he strip. And since Amy was super hot, and since he was confused and horny, things happened.

Jake isn't obtuse. He labored under no delusions about love. He knew good and well Amy just wanted to get back at David, and was well aware she didn't have any real feelings for him. He loves Melanie. Events just got out of hand. He let his desires get the better of him.

All the same Jake tries not to beat himself up over the whole thing. Frankly, he's not blind to the part of Melanie that seems to be pulling away. He suspects Melanie and him might have the same dilemma; namely, feelings for Amy. There seem to be no good feelings really left between the two of them.

So why is he so terrified of being alone? He thinks he knows why. *What if it happens again*? he wonders. He'd barely survived the last time. He isn't stable enough to be on his own. But he can't be totally honest with anyone. Of course not. *Christ, they'd have me committed. They'd put me in the funny farm fast as you could say dude, you're crazy.*

David might have been loaded as fuck at that party, but Jake had only been moderately buzzed. He'd seen everything: the kiss on the stairs between Melanie, and Amy. He has felt the weight of that kiss for months now, like some feral creature hanging on his back, clawing at him. A creature that doesn't care about his life, or his well being. A creature that only wants to rip, and tear, and destroy the thing it has a hold of.

If he could just get his fucking shit together and tell Melanie the truth, maybe things could be okay. If he could tell her why he had done what he had done; explain to her none of this was her fault, that he was a complete and utter trash fire. If only he could tell them all about what happened in the desert years ago; why he woke most nights in a cold sweat, afraid he might have screamed and woke the neighbors, or Melanie herself in bed beside him.

There's a grey cat rubbing against the leg of his jeans. *When in the hell did that—*

"What the fuck?"

"Aw, kitty," Melanie says, reaching out and petting the little grey cat.

"Where the fuck did that cat come from?" David asks, smoking a joint.

"When did you start… You know what, nevermind. Pass that." David sticks out his tongue between an exhalation of weed smoke. He does pass the joint over to Jake, who greedily drags.

"It has a collar," Amy says, squinting down at the tag. "I can't read it, anyone got a flashlight?"

"Yeah," Melanie says. She rummages through her bag, and finds a plastic ziploc bag full of a flashlight, a first aid kit, and various other toiletries such as a toothbrush, and toothpaste. She pulls out the flashlight, hands it to Amy, who clicks it on, and points the beam at the little metal tag on the cat's black collar.

"Says hear her name is 'Lillie.'"

"She's cute," Jake says, also petting the grey cat.

"You guys are dumb," David says. Then he loudly farts.

"I fucking hate you," Jake says, sighing. "Amy, can I kill him yet?"

"Give it a day," Amy says, opening a new beer with a crack of the top of the can, foam pouring onto her fingers. She licks the foam from the top of her thumb, and catches Jake's eyes. He can't tell if she's into him staring, or not. He decides to stop staring; his instincts are even if she is into it it's a creepy thing to do.

The little grey cat curls up in the dirt by the fire, and nestles its tiny feline head against its forepaws. Jake can't remember what he was thinking about, and ultimately decides *screw it, I'm likely better off not dwelling on things I can't change.*

So he watches the cat, and the campfire, and drinks from his beer, smokes another hit off the joint. He places his hand in Melanie's, who smiles and gives him a peck on the cheek. He feels his heart ache for her, knowing she isn't happy.

Jake hasn't been anything close to happy in years. Happiness is like some cryptid he can never seem to prove exists. Joy is a very distant memory, from sometime before he enlisted. From his time before Desert Storm.

He drinks his beer faster.

A few hours and many empty beer cans later Melanie is pleasantly buzzed, the feeling of lightheadedness like floating as a peaceful spirit; all is right with the world, her secret desires momentarily checked. A smile from ear to ear she can feel practically hurts her face.

The little grey cat is still snuggled by the fire. Jake is smiling, laughing, hugging her, spilling beer onto the front of his Soundgarden t-shirt, and when did he even put that on, wasn't he wearing a flannel before? She can't seem to remember, not exactly blackout, but not quite point A to point B in a straight line. Frames are missing from her movie, the editor showing off with some choppy cutting.

For just a moment, Melanie feels like someone is watching her. She pushes the feelings aside, thinking *I'm just absolutely loaded. I could feel any number of things that would prove to be wrong.* She swears she hears a whisper from behind her, a voice saying sweetly, *you won't ever leave this place.* Being belligerent as fuck, she gives Jake a dead arm.

"Ah, what was that for?"

"Don't whisper… creepy things, creepy man," she says, words stumbling out as wobbly as she herself is, the world lightly spinning.

Amy throws an empty at Jake. It smacks him square in the mouth.

"The fuck is wrong with you?" Jake yells.

"Don't be man creepy!" she yells back, then belches.

"Woah, this is like, fucking hostile," David says, speaking through a haze of weed smoke.

"Jesus, man, don't smoke all the weed in one night," Jake says, giving David the finger. Jake stares at the fire, apparently having given up trying to keep out of his own head, or at least this is what it seems like to Melanie, who is, as established, pretty darn blotto.

Melanie can tell something is bothering him, but as always she isn't sure what to do. Jake has this ability to seem like a sad sack on seemingly happy occasions, and boy, is she one to talk. After all, she is pining after Amy from one kiss, a kiss that to Amy likely amounted to just some fun thing on Halloween, but has ended up growing to mythic proportions inside of her own head. Dare she think it, but the words come unbidden and unwanted, *I am hopelessly in love with Amy. I want to wake up with her beside me every day. And there's not a chance in hell she reciprocates.*

This seems to be Melanie's lot in life. Falling for the wrong people. Making rash decisions based on her emotional whims. She feels like a yippy puppy around Amy, all unbridled energy that never dissipates. She's sure she comes off like a super annoying clingy-ditz.

"Where's the weirdest place you've had sex?" Amy asks Melanie.

Melanie freezes like a deer in the headlights, as if Amy can somehow hear her thoughts.

"I um… like…"

"Oh, come on Melanie! We're all friends here. Spill it. What's the strangest place you've fucked?"

"Well, uh… I, um… had sex in a bathroom at a Friendly's, once."

"Dang!" David says, his eyes going wide in a way Melanie isn't exactly thrilled about.

"Well, what about you, pervo?" Melanie asks, staring pointedly across the fire at David. "Where's the weirdest place you've made the beast with two backs?"

"There were three backs, and it was in an alley outside a nightclub in Boston."

"Gross," Melanie says, and she looks over at Amy to gauge her reaction, but she can't see her face well enough in the semi-glow of the lightly flaming campfire.

"I once did it at a roller rink," Amy says.

"What? Roller Kingdom?" Jake asks.

"Yeah."

"So, like, in the bathroom, right?" David asks.

"No. I knew a guy that worked there. He had keys so I snuck in one night, and we banged on the middle of the roller rink."

"Grimy!" Jake says, laughing.

"I once had sex in a church," Jake says, and David gets real animated at this, hooting practically chimp-like, "ooohhhhhh, oh man, when?!"

"Few years ago. It was a Catholic church in, like, I think it was Wareham?"

"What, western Mass?"

"Yeah."

"The fuck were you doing in western mass, that's like, hours from where you live."

"I was getting my johnson wet."

"Oh my God, Jake, please never call it your 'johnson,' again," Melanie says, visibly bristling.

"I thought you liked my…" and at this Jake leans in to whisper "johnson."

"EW! I want to fucking die, babe," Melanie says, mock dry heaving. She is actually very grossed out, mostly from hearing about Jake fucking in a church. She's not exactly religious, but it just seems disrespectful. It doesn't *seem* disrespectful, it is disrespectful, like, totally fucking disrespectful.

"Yup. I turned my No Fear hat backwards, dropped my plaid shorts, and proceeded to make sweet monkey love to —"

"To who?" Melanie asks.

Jake finally seems to remember he's sitting next to his girlfriend, and lowers the volume of his voice. He quietly says "nobody you'd know."

The night slowly meanders on like an old cow with an inner ear problem. The beer can tops crack open, the fizz of the escaping air like the dying breath of a liquid being. Melanie goes from fun drunk to melancholy drunk (as she is wont to do) and turns to her favorite topic of conversation.

"Do you think Nirvana would have got bad if Kurt hadn't killed himself?"

All the rest groan, and David actually boos. She flips them all the bird, and takes out a Marlboro Light.

"I thought you quit smoking," Jake says, not a question, a statement. He's smoking a Marlboro Red himself. *Hypocrite*, she thinks.

"Yeah, well, one every once and a while won't kill me."

"I mean, it actually will, but whatever, do what you want."

He takes a long drag off his cigarette. "Jackass," Melanie mumbles, ashing out her cancer stick in the dirt. "Anyway, I mean it. Do you think Nirvana would have got bad if Kurt had lived and they kept making music?"

"What, like, as in would they have made a new album around now or last year that was bad?"

"Well, yes, but also, going forward, into the 2000s and stuff."

"Melanie, who can predict what the hell music is going to be like in the 2000s," Amy says. "If Nirvana would even still be making music."

David pulls an OK Soda out of his bag.

"Shit, did you bring any more of those?" Jake asks.

"Nope," David says, opening the can of fructose syrup infused soda, and drinking deeply. He burps, loud and long.

"No one is answering my question," Melanie says, forlorn, the sad drunk, just trying to get anyone to listen to her. "What do—"

"I'm just going to say it," Jake interjects, cutting her off. "I never really loved Nirvana." His cigarette now down to the filter, he flicks it into the fire.

Melanie's whole body jolts back, as if she's just been slapped.

"Who doesn't like Nirvana?!"

"Oh my God, Mel, plenty of people don't like the band."

"Yeah, stupid people!"

"Okay, okay, break it up, you two," Amy says, frowning. "I'll answer the question, though for the record, I have answered this question over and over. Mel, you always get too drunk to remember."

"Well?"

"I think they were a lightning in a bottle band. They showed up at the right time, got a smash hit, and then Kurt ended up offing himself before they could have the inevitable decline that most bands experience. So, yes, I think Nirvana would have eventually become worse, and would have made a lot more albums people decidedly did not like."

The rain has entirely stopped now, save little drizzles. Melanie lights another cigarette just to spite Jake. The smoke in her lungs feels like a sort of religious ritual, sacrament; exhaling slowly, the chemicals and tobacco filling her head with a buzz, filling her body with cancer-forming residue.

"I think they would have kept making great music," Melanie slurs out.

"Hey, you're entitled to that," Jake says.

"Fuck you!" Melanie slurs at him.

"Chill out, I'm fucking agreeing with you, you drunken idiot."

"Oh," Melanie says, then hiccups. "I shoud go to bed."

"I think we all should," Amy says.

"Sounds good," David says, then grabs a bucket of water close to the fire to drown out the flames.

Flashlight beams click on, and David and Jake go to their respective tents. Melanie still sits on the log. Amy walks over to her.

"Hey, what's up—"

Amy kisses her deeply on the mouth. Melanie feels her body sink into the heat of Amy's, arms entangling, moisture of lips commingling; the universe shrinks to the space around just the two of them, sinking into a black hole of lust, passion, and yearning. And just like that, what feels like a veritable implosion as Amy pulls away, and calls out to David "Sorry, I forgot my shirt!" and Melanie is left dazed and confused in the darkness, biting her lip, wondering now if she'll ever be able to get any sleep.

The next morning Jake feels sort of hungover. He isn't sure if Melanie was whispering in her sleep, but he heard a woman's voice whispering last night. The young woman's voice sounded like it was close to the tent. Maybe Amy was sleepwalking? Who the hell knows.

Being the first to wake Jake gets the fire going—a markedly easier endeavor this morning not having the rain. The ground is drier than when they first arrived. *Thank the universe for small favors,* he thinks. He manages to get the flame to a few inches off some dry twigs he brought in a plastic baggy he pre-packed, and a piece of fatwood. He does have lighter fluid if he needs it; he's good, but he's not so proud he won't cheat. Work smarter, not harder and all that.

He opens the cooler to get the eggs (ridiculous for them to bring eggs, but they are in a special container and appear to not have cracked) and some bacon (bacon is smoked so there's a greater chance for it to stay fresh). While Jake gets the fire to a good cooking temp, adding small sticks, and a tiny bit of charcoal he's brought in his wetbag, he thinks about Amy. He wonders if Melanie has any idea of his feelings for his best friend's girl, or if she even cares; his girlfriend seems so very disinterested in him, as of late. He stares at the crackling flames and lets his mind wander.

He's known Amy the longest out of all of them. Jake remembers his first day of second grade, in a new school, talking to Amy in the way boys and girls did before puberty hit and all the hormones got in the way. He stayed fairly good friends with Amy over the years. She may not be a best friend, or even in his top 5 friends, yet they have a solid friendship.

A switch flipped after they had sex, a circuit breaker turned on; electricity newly rushing to the part of his memories labeled "Amy." He wishes he could stop the feelings. He can't. And it makes Jake retroactively rethink every single fucking interaction they've ever had together.

He loves Melanie. At least, he's pretty sure that he does. So, why the incredible doubt?

"Do I smell bacon and eggs?" David says behind him. He nearly falls into the fire.

"Fuck! Dude, a little warning next time!"

"What? I'm not cumming in your mouth, I'm just saying good morning."

"Something smells good," Amy says, yawning.

"Ugh, food," is all Melanie says, rummaging through her wet bag for a Pop Tart.

"What, ya hungover?" David asks.

"No shit, sherlock."

"Hey, no reason for the 'tude."

"I'll show you fucking 'tude, dumbass," Melanie says, shaking her fist at David. The gesture is only a little bit playful, Jake can tell.

"I was thinking we could go for a canoe trip, then a hike later on," Amy says. She looks expectantly at the rest of them.

"Yeah, that could be fun," Jake says, staring Amy in her eyes, trying to gauge her expression.

What is she thinking? Is she thinking of me? Why do I even care? She probably doesn't ever think about me. I'm probably just some dweeb in the corner to her, some asshole on the periphery. A woman like that can have her pick. She doesn't want me.

They eat in silence, on plastic bowls with camping silverware. The food is good, Jake has to admit. He's always been a fairly good cook. And this is not just something his mother told him, complete strangers have told him this when he's thrown backyard BBQs at the house David rents in Framingham. And he's always enjoyed cooking for people; he gets the same joy out of it he gets out of pleasing people sexually, or making someone's day in some other such way, like helping them with their groceries, or helping them move.

One character flaw he is admittedly guilty of is obsession. He hates not knowing, and this relates to anything. He loathes not knowing how people feel, or what they think of him. There's ultimately nothing Jake can do about this, but it doesn't stop him from getting neurotic.

"Hey. Serious face."

It's Melanie, looking slightly better from when he first saw her when she woke up.

"What is it?"

"It's not the end of the world, dude."

"What isn't?"

"Whatever is making you make that face. Come on."

And at this, Melanie takes his hand. "Let's go for a hike."

"You sure you're up for it?"

"Eh, I could use a cig anyway," Melanie says.

"Butt head."

"Takes one to know one," Melanie says. She smiles at him in a strange way.

He isn't sure what to make of it.

Ten minutes later they fuck among the trees, Melanie with her face against a pine tree as Jake takes her from behind. Her mind turns to Amy, and she lets it. *No law against going where your mind takes you*, Melanie thinks. Everything feels good, it's helping her with her hangover, or at least getting her mind off her headache.

"Yeah, you like that?" Jake says, panting behind her.

"Yes," she says, annoyed for his intrusion into her mental gymnastics to picture herself with Amy.

"You want me to—"

"Shhhh," she says, placing her finger to his lips, behind her.

She thrusts her hips backwards, and hears Jake groan, then feels the wetness sliding down her inner thigh.

Damn it, she thinks, placing her middle finger on her clit, rubbing in a circle. She'd been so close, and now she thinks of Amy and their kiss last Halloween, and the way Amy looks in her jeans, and their kiss yesterday, and all at once her legs are having trouble holding her as the waves of pleasure crash into her. And she falls to her knees, panting, lying next to the pine tree.

"Sorry," Jake says, sullenly.

"It's fine, Jake," she says, and it is now, because she finished the job.

A rustling among the trees to her left and she darts a quick glance. Melanie can't see any animal. "Damn it, Jake, tell me you heard that?"

"What's that, babe?"

Oh for fuck's sake.

"Christ, nevermind, let's just head back to camp."

"Cig first," Jake says, fishing a Marlboro Red out of his pack, lighting it with a white lighter.

"Is that your lighter?" Melanie asks.

"I... think so?" Jake says, pulling off that cigarette, exhaling, inspecting the white Bic lighter in his hand. "If it isn't, I'm not sure whose it is."

Melanie lights her own cig, gently lowering herself to the forest floor beside him. They smoke in silence, staring off at the trees.

An hour passes. Amy and the rest have the canoes out on the water. Amy forgot who suggested this. *Did I suggest this?* Her memory can be terrible, sometimes. All the drinking has certainly not helped.

The day is overcast, grey like stones, clouds like ripped cotton. There is a stillness to Lake George that Amy enjoys, one she rarely gets; a silence and calmness living with David definitely never allows her. Living with David is sort of like living with a strange, horny, hairless ape with the ability to talk: one that talks way too much, at that.

Should I tell him about Melanie? Should I tell him about Jake?

She knows what David will do. David is nothing if not predictable. He'll shout and call her a "whore," and a "bitch," and maybe even the c word. Which is totally not fair, because he is, after all, the asshole that caused her to cheat in the first place, by sticking his dick into anything with a pulse.

You're on vacation, just deal with all this bullshit later, Amy thinks.

So she takes in the wilderness all about them, and a short time later David hands her a joint she happily puffs away at. A hawk flies overhead, crying out, and she watches with a smile as large fish jump out of the surface of the lake. The waves aren't bad today, for whatever reason most of the speed boats seem to have taken the day off.

She wonders if Melanie likes her. Amy does like Melanie, but she's a little confused about everything. She never thought she was into women. It wasn't like she was a closeted lesbian, or anything. The idea had never really crossed her path until last Halloween.

Amy hears the hawk scream. She feels the motion as the bird dive bombs her, claws scratching at her outstretched hand as she blocks her face.

"NO!" she yells, grabbing her canoe paddle and raising it like a weapon.

"Shit," David says, paddling for the closest shore.

The hawk cries out again, eyes wide in aggression; the bird swooping down, claws outstretched. Amy swings the paddle into the bird, and direct hit, feathers flying, the bird falling into the water; getting its bearings, then taking off into the trees on the opposite shore to where they paddle the canoe. The hawk disappears into the tree line.

"What the hell was that?" Amy yells, wincing as she grabs the emergency first aid kit they keep in the canoe. She pours antiseptic into the wound, and grits her teeth from the pain, watching the wound on her hand foam.

"That bird of prey fucking preyed on us!" David yells, then laughs.

"I am well aware, David!" Amy rubs ointment onto the wound, which is thankfully not bleeding all that much, and doesn't hurt too badly. Thank the Norse gods.

Melanie and Jake pull their canoe up a minute later, Melanie rushing out of the boat to hug Amy.

"Are you okay?"

"I'm all right, Mel."

"What was with that bird?!"

"I have no idea," Amy says, "one minute it looked chill, then the next it was out for blood."

"Well, do you still want to hike?" Jake asks.

Amy thinks everything over, and ultimately decides, "what the heck, we're already here, let's enjoy the sights."

"Fucking birds, man," David says, seemingly to no one.

The trees seem to sigh all around them, and David wonders if it's going to rain. The wind whispering through the hemlocks like a small child sneaking around the house. Pine needles and leaves litter the ground and crunch underfoot with stones and sticks, a soundtrack to their travels, crunch, crunch.

"It's really pretty out here," David says to Amy, who just gives him a thumbs up. He knows her well enough to know she's in a lot of pain, so he rummages through his pocket, and produces a baggy of pills.

"Pain killer?"

"What kind?"

"Nothing too heavy. Tylenol 3. Some Vics."

"Give me a few Vics."

"Sure thing, my love."

David shakes two Vicodin out of the plastic baggy into Amy's good hand. She takes the pills and tosses them back with gusto, snatching David's water bottle to down the little white painkillers.

"Salud," David says, and Amy just sighs.

"I know you slept around," she finally says.

Davis isn't sure what to say, so he says nothing. Amy is the first to reply after some moments of them hiking on, the others far enough behind they've heard none of it. "We'll deal with all of this when the trip is over. For now, just, try to act normal. Don't cause a scene."

David just sighs and says "yeah." He stares into the rain, letting the cool water wet his brow. He likes the sensation.

They continue the hike, the sky growing progressively darker; an inkwell tipped onto a grey-blue rug. On the way back, David feels the strain in his knees and the bottom of his feet (he should have worn the hiking boots instead of the Vans, after all). He hears the crows before seeing them in their full glory. The murder stands atop a deer carcass, one greedy little corvid ripping the left eye out of the animal's head.

Melanie projectile vomits off the side of the trail.

"That's fucked," Melanie says, wiping puke from around her mouth.

"That poor deer," Jake says, horrified.

"Can we please just go?" Amy asks. The rest agree they should leave.

They head back to the boats, perhaps a little faster than their walk in.

It's early evening when Jake works the fire back up to cook the stew, using pre-cooked stew beef he's stored in the cooler. He throws baby potatoes, carrots, a little bit of red wine from a bottle he uncorks, and beef broth from the cooler. Melanie is absolutely starving. She could eat a horse. Thinking of a horse makes her think of the dead deer, and she shudders.

"Well, who wants to get drinking?" David asks.

"Me," Melanie says, lifting her hand.

"We're not in school dude, you don't have to raise your hand," Jake says, stirring the stew. Shrugging, then pouring a little more red wine into the pot.

"Yay, poison!" Amy says, laughing.

This time some red wine out of red plastic cups, though beer certainly flows. Melanie feels the wine go straight to her cheeks, a pleasant warmth inside of her, particularly in her lower extremities. She figures it must be a Celtic thing to go a bit red in the face. *Maybe, who even knows*. Melanie has no real idea.

"Who wants to go fishing?" David asks.

"With what?" Amy asks, giving David a face like she just smelled cat shit.

"Oh, I brought poles."

"Get out of town," Jake says.

"Hey, what goes better than drinking and fishing?"

"Not drowning to death?" Melanie says, a strain in her voice.

She tries to keep them from leaving. She obviously fails.

Melanie and David fish off the rocky shore, sky a golden orange hue like the embers of a long-burning fire, coals a hot bed in the tinted blue of the heavens. Melanie and David laugh as they reel in, and cast the fishing lines in the placid water. Amy sits by Jake, and they are far enough back she knows the others can't hear.

"Look, Jake, I've been meaning to talk to you."

"Yes?" Jake knows to expect the worst when he looks into Amy's eyes, the way the sadness tints them.

"That was a mistake, okay? What we did. I was just trying to get back at David."

"I sort of suspected that."

"Look, you're a great guy, and Melanie is crazy about you."

"Ha."

"What's that supposed to mean?"

"She wants you, Amy. She doesn't even like me anymore."

"Oh, Jake."

Tears stream down Jake's face. *Pull yourself together, dude. Don't make a scene.*

"Are you okay?" Amy asks, putting her hand on his arm. He pulls his arm away, quickly, like her touch burns. In many ways it does.

"I sort of figured that. Reality Bites, that's for sure."

"Jesus dude, can you find a less organic way to throw in a reference?"

Amy laughs, staring off towards the lake. Jake watches the blue of her eyes and wishes he didn't ache seeing those eyes.

"Clerks, Surge, Co-Ed Naked," he blurts out.

"I was kidding, Jake."

"That is Jacob to you."

"Is it, though?"

"No, I'm just a bit drunk, I'm sorry."

"Oh, honey."

Amy leans in and hugs Jake. Jake begrudgingly accepts the hug. He's too broken to fight anymore.

On the shore, Melanie laughs as she reels in, fishing rod in her drunken hands. David is just being a stupid asshole (as usual) shimmying as he reels in his line. She likes David but he can also annoy the ever loving shit out of her. Thankfully, this is not one of those times.

"This is actually kinda fun," she says, reeling in the line, little silver lure coming free of the water. She flicks the bail arm over to place her finger on the line itself, then casts off with all her might, letting go of the line just as gravity starts to hurl the lure towards the lake.

"It is a ton of fun," David says. "People think fishing is for old people, but it really can be a blast."

"Are we even allowed to fish here?"

David gives her an exaggerated shrug of his shoulders that nearly makes him fall over in his wasted state. *That's our David,* Melanie thinks, giggling.

All of a sudden Melanie's line has an incredible tug. Melanie launches off of her feet and falls chest first onto the sand.

"Holy shit!" David says. He drops to his knees to grab the pole from Melanie, and she watches as he seems to reel in the line with relative ease. David cranks the line out of the water. The lure has been bitten off.

"Whoa."

"Is that normal?" Melanie asks from the ground.

"I mean, in a lake, I don't know. This line is pretty strong."

"So that's not normal."

"It's definitely super weird. Yeah."

Melanie feels a chill work its way up her spine.

Whatever it was, it must have been big.

The sun is setting when they get back to camp. Jake works the fire up again, having put it out earlier when they left. Amy drinks what she thinks is her third cup of red wine, but she has honestly forgot how many it's been.

This whole situation is such a mess, she thinks. *I don't know if I like Amy or not, it's so muddled in my head. But I know I don't want to date Jake, or David for that matter. Christ, why do men have to be so fucking stupid all the time?*

Amy supposes this maybe isn't fair to Jake. Yeah, David is an asshole who can rot, but Jake didn't do anything wrong. Except, she realizes he did actually do *a lot* wrong. He cheated on one of her best friends. And he cheated on one of her friends *with* her, so he was far from blameless. She had a reason to cheat, that's how she justifies everything. But Jake? Jake was with Melanie, who was such a sweet, caring, funny, charming, witty woman.

Anyone should be happy as fuck to be with Melanie, she thinks. *Hell, I would.*

She's so fucking confused. It's probably all the wine. Even still, her Freudian slip appears to be showing. She downs the rest of her plastic cup of red. Her mind racing, her heart thumping in her chest.

"Okay, I got one for y'all," Jake drunkenly slurs.

"When did you become southern?" David drunkenly asks.

"You shut up!" Amy drunkenly interjects. She slurs, "go on Jake, what's yer question?"

"How'd ya know it was a question?" he asks, eyes half-focused.

"Just go, ya silly!" Amy shouts, loudly.

"Would you rather have bad sex for the rest of your life, or have to eat shit?"

"What, like, eat shit regularly and often?" David asks. He belches.

"No, just the one time."

"Oh, no contest," David says. "Bring on the Poo Poo platter."

"Fucking gross, David," Amy says.

"Okay, what about drinking pee, or bad sex for the next 20 years?"

"Jake, really, I think you should stop with these questions," Melanie says. Amy can tell Mel is past tired of all these weird hypotheticals they all keep spouting.

"Well? What is it to be, then?" Jake asks. He finishes his beer in one gulp, then crushes the can under his boot.

Melanie sighs.

"How much pee?"

"Like, pee once a week for 5 years."

"Or bad sex for 20?"

"Yup."

"Well, who knows what life can bring you. Fuck it, I'm drinking piss for 5 years, and enjoying 20 years of carnal delights."

Amy notes Melanie makes deliberate eye contact when she says this last part about carnal delights. Amy can feel herself blushing. She starts to imagine scenarios in her head with Melanie. Maybe later tonight, when the boys are asleep. Or, hell, maybe with the boys. She's in the sort of mood she gets into often, what she thinks of as her "fuck it," mood. Essentially, if there's anyone she likes around... well, "fuck it."

"Okay, here's one," Melanie says. "Would you rather lose an arm, or a leg?"

"Hmm," Amy says. "That's tough. I think a leg, because it'd be harder to do anything with one arm."

"But they have the prosthetics, like, the hook and stuff," Jake drunkenly slurs.

"I'm saying leg," David says. "I like being able to play with my marbles with both hands."

"Eloquent, as ever," Melanie says, pouring more red into her plastic cup.

Melanie doesn't need a mirror to know her cheeks are rosy: red wine does this to her. And frankly, she does not care. She thinks Amy might be down to fool around later. *Down to clown around*, she thinks, and giggles.

"Actually, I've changed my mind," Amy says. "I have nice legs."

"Yeah you *really* do," Melanie says, and it takes her a beat before she realizes she's said this out loud, and tries to course correct with "girlfriend," and inwardly she's cursing herself for being such a drunken moron.

"Now the big question, the biggest to me," Jake says, "Is: would you rather lose the left one or the right one?"

"What are you asking?" Amy says.

"Well, for the guys, the left or right—"

"Oh dang, do you mean which nut?" Jake says, perhaps a bit louder than he intended, Melanie thinks.

"Yeah, dude," David says.

"I think the right one," Jake says. "I heard the left one has more jizz in it."

"Wow, okay," Amy says, laughing. "I thought David was the idiot."

"Oh, fuck off," Jake says, and Melanie can tell by his tone he's only half-kidding.

"That's the most ridiculous god damn thing I've ever heard," Melanie says, deadpan. She flips Jake the bird. He in turn also flips her off.

"Why the left one?" Amy asks.

"I tend to sleep on my left side," Jake says. "I won't have to worry about squishing it between my legs as often."

"Does that happen a lot, honey?" Melanie asks.

"I mean, define 'a lot'?"

"Well, okay, OKAY!" David yells, "ladies, right or left boob?"

"Ah, okay, I see now," Melanie says. "This is a conundrum."

"My right one is bigger," Amy says, "so I'm getting rid of lefty."

"I can't believe we're having this conversation," Melanie says, about to pour the rest of the bottle of red into her cup, shrugging, then drinking straight from the bottle.

"So, Mel, which titty is going on the chopping block?" David says, slurring out the back half of the sentence into almost imperceptible gibberish.

"Oh God, don't say it like that…"

"Well, let's hear it, woman."

"I'm actually also voting for my left," Melanie says. "No real reason. I'm right handed, so, I guess get rid of my opposite boob?"

"Okay, here's one," Amy says. "If you were able to clone yourself, would you want to fuck yourself?"

"Oh, absolutely!" David says with drunken enthusiasm.

"Well, which one of you would be the one getting penetrated?" Amy says, and the look on David's face lets her know this question snuck up on him.

"Woah! Like, in the butt? Obviously my clone, dude. The back is strictly exit only."

"It wasn't that one time when I stuck my finger in your —" Amy begins, but David interrupts quickly with "what about you Jake?"

"Well, what if you were the clone?" Jake asks.

"Why would I be the clone?" David says.

"I don't know, in this case, you just, like, are."

"Huh… I mean, I don't really want to get fucked. Maybe I'd blow me. That seems like a good compromise."

"Would you swallow?" Amy asks, genuinely curious.

"Spitters are quitters, as they says," David drunkenly slurs out.

"As who says?" Amy asks.

"What about you, Amy?" Melanie asks.

"Oh, yup, I'd jump my bones, do all manner of perversions to my duplicate."

"I think we're all in agreement we'd mess around with our clones," Amy says.

"Hey, I never said I would."

There's a silence for a bit. Smiles on all their faces, Melanie included. She's feeling warm: from the fire, from the alcohol. *This is nice*, she thinks, and looks over at Amy. They lock eyes, and for just a moment Melanie can see the desire writ large upon her face; she might as well have big flashing lights and arrows.

"I got one," Jake says, a strange grin upon his face Melanie can't quite suss out.

"If you could be a ghost, and like, possess someone's body, who would it be and what would you do?" Jake pulls out a new Marlboro Red, lights it with a white Bic lighter flame that can't seem to hit the target of the end of the cigarette.

"Oh, man, this is getting outlandish!" David yells, laughing.

"I think I'd possess Michelle Pfeiffer," Melanie says.

"And do what?" Amy asks.

"Um…" Melanie blushes.

"I think we all know what she's going to do," Jake says, giving her a wink.

"No, not necessarily *just* that."

"Okay, I got one." David says. "I'd possess Amy."

"Me?"

"Yeah, and then I'd look at myself in the mirror, all naked, and stuff."

"Is that all we're going to go straight to? Who would you possess to fuck or masturbate as?" Melanie says.

Amy, David, and Jake all reply in unison "yes."

"You guys suck," Melanie says, sighing theatrically. "Let's get to some stuff that isn't sex related, *for a change.*"

"Well, like what?" Amy asks.

"Like, if you could die, but you knew you would come back in a few minutes, would you want to?"

There's a silence after this question, only the flames of the fire and the crickets chirping, and the rustling of the wind through the leaves. Amy stares at David, at Melanie. She holds her gaze on Jake. She wishes Melanie hadn't brought up the question. Especially considering what he'd tried to do all that time ago.

"I think I would, yeah," David says, sipping his beer, while the others stare on, solemnly.

"So you're not afraid of dying?" Jake asks.

"Oh, of course I'm afraid of dying. But it'd be rad to actually know what happens."

"I don't think I want to know," Melanie says.

"I don't know if I want to either," Jake says. "I would hate it to just be darkness, you know, just blackness, and nothing. I'd rather not know if it's just going to be that."

"So you're not curious?" Melanie asks.

Amy quietly curses Melanie thinking *Jesus, change the fucking subject!*

"Oh, yes, but not enough to die, even if I knew I'd come back a few minutes later," Jake says.

"And what about you, Amy? You want to die if you can come right back?" Melanie asks.

"Shit… I don't know. I'm pretty drunk and this is a little out of my range right now, Mel."

"Who wants to have a sing along?"

"Holy shit, what?"

"I brought the boom box, and got a few cassettes."

An hour later and another case of beer opened, Jake nearly falls over as he stands to sing the chorus of Pearl Jam's "I'm Still Alive." The music cranks from the Sony boombox, in such a way that none of them, including Jake, hear the thing that stands just out of the fire's light. A thing of rotting skin, blue-purple-green decaying flesh; gangrenous and dangerous, a nasty implement of destruction in its red right hand. A weapon of doom, currently silent, waiting, oiled and at the ready like a soldier in war paint. The thing in the shadows of the trees is oozing as well, though not with oil, fluids such as puss; butyric fermentation, acids eating through the remaining dripping, mushy flesh.

If Jake was not so loaded (or indeed if any of the rest of them were not) they would likely smell the pungent reek of death that pervades the air, but perhaps the constant breeze upon Lake George would cover it up. Who can really say.

The thing licks its lips, so bloated from putrefaction any semblance of humanity now only found in the eyes, bloodshot and decayed, a yellowish tint; large tears in the corneas, puss like tears sliding down the cheeks, which expose teeth and jaw bones from the right angle, such is the lack of connective tissue left from the rigors of death.

Soon enough, the dead man with the chainsaw will let his blade speak for him.

It certainly wouldn't be the first time.

The orgy occurs seemingly out of nowhere, for the most part prompted by Amy, Amy thinking to herself *fuck the world, I'm going to have some fun this vacation. I'm not getting any younger.* If any of it had been pre-planned, the group sex likely would not have occurred. Such events need an element of spontaneity to them, for the most part.

Amy starts by having sex with David, and then she does what she's wanted to do all weekend. Amy kisses Melanie deeply on the mouth, their tongues intertwining, hands exploring each others' bodies. This is the part of the orgy Amy loves, though the rest isn't so bad, either. She's never been someone to let emotions get in the way of pleasure, at least not all the time, but she finds the passion between Melanie and herself enhancing what is otherwise sort of meaningless but pleasurable fucking with Jake, and then David again.

For her part Melanie has sex with Jake, and Amy (again) but only with David for a little, though by this point David appears to be fairly spent so he just watches as Jake, Amy, and Melanie finish messing around with each other.

Afterwards, dragging on a cigarette, Amy stares at the stars in the sky, feeling the aftershocks rumble through her body, sitting on a log she's pulled over by the fire. Melanie is lying on the ground, Mad Season t-shirt on but nothing else, David and Jake shirtless, but with their pants on. David is the first to speak, and in typical fashion, the conversation is out of nowhere.

"Why is Garfield always such a fucking dickhead?"

"Oh my God, this is what you want to talk about?" Melanie says from her place on the ground, by the fire. "We just had a fucking orgy and you want to talk about Garfield?"

"I mean, what is there to talk about? We were horny, so we fucked. All the rest is just, I don't know, periphery."

Melanie stands, slowly, walks over to her jeans lying on the ground and pulls them on, not bothering to put her underwear back on. *Commando* she thinks, and giggles.

"I guess you're right," Amy says, hesitantly, looking over and Melanie, feeling the love growing inside of her, unsure if she likes the feeling.

"Anyway, where was I… oh yes, Garfield."

"Holy shit dude, shut up, I'm trying to enjoy my postcoital haze," Jake says.

"No, honestly? I get that he's a cat, and the joke is that cats are mean, but Garfield is, like, pathological."

"Well, he hates Mondays."

"Oh, that's not all. Have you seen his attitude to Odie, or God forbid, Nermal?"

"Damn guys, I might fucking sleep, I can't handle anymore Garfield conversation right now," Jake says. He lights another Red, sticks the cigarette in his mouth. Takes a large drag, exhales a massive cloud of smoke.

David keeps rambling on about Garfield, but Amy notices Melanie get up, to sit next to her on the log. Melanie kisses her, hard on the mouth, her tongue running along her own, David watching in stunned silence.

"Whoa. Are you guys lesbos?"

"No, Dave, we just love kissing and fucking each other."

"Is this why you're breaking up with me?"

"What? No. You cheated on me a shitload, asshole."

"Well… I will neither confirm nor deny that…"

"What does it matter if I am gay," Amy says, not a question, a statement, one she's thinking out loud.

I mean my parents will likely disown me, and I'll lose friends, and gain new stigmas. I'll have to reevaluate who I am as a person, maybe, or maybe not, I have no idea. Do I have to butch up, or can I stay how I am, or…

Amy quickly realizes being gay will change a lot of her life, and she hopes it's for the better, but she just doesn't know. Maybe she should have stayed closeted? *You know, because bottling up desire always works so well for people.* Amy looks into the lines of Melanie's face, the freckles she has she tries to cover up; she wishes Melanie would stop doing that, her freckles are beautiful. *Melanie is beautiful* she thinks. *I could spend the rest of my life with her.* And then the panic sings deep inside. What is she going to do? Amy has no real idea, yet, so she tries to push the worry down deep, hidden inside.

"Look, I just want to know what the hell is going on," David says, a little heat in his voice now. "If you want to be a dyke, that's fine."

"Don't fucking call me that," Amy says, now angry. "That's not a nice word."

"What, dyke? Well you are a dyke, you fucking dyke."

"Oh, stop being a child," Amy says, shaking another cigarette out of her pack, and lighting up, angrily taking her first inhale. She looks over at Melanie, who suddenly looks very sad.

"I love Melanie," Amy says. It feels good to finally express this out loud.

Melanie, beside her, audibly gasps.

"What did you say?"

She turns to Melanie, running her hand along her cheek.

"I… love you," Amy says.

A smile lights up Melanie's face, and she darts in to kiss Amy, her movement so quick the two of them topple off of the log, and land hard onto the ground. Amy feels her knee connect with Mel's crotch on the way down, and hears the sound she makes, a sort of "oof," noise.

"Aw, shit," Melanie says, grabbing her crotch through her jeans.

"Oh my God, Mel, I'm so sorry," Amy says, laughing a bit.

"Ow, it's fine, Amy," Melanie says, though her facial expression shows Amy she's in some pain.

"Direct contact?"

"Oh yeah," Melanie says, standing gingerly.

"Does that hurt women?" David asks.

"What, getting kneed in the vagina? Of course it fucking hurts," Melanie says. "Would it hurt if I wailed you in the butthole?"

"Yeah, I guess," David says.

"Well, there you go, it's the same basic principle, just more sensitive," Mel says, grabbing a half full can of beer off the ground, and drinking it down in one big gulp. She throws the empty can behind her back.

"Okay, litterbug," David says.

"I'll pick it up tomorrow, you nag," Melanie says.

"Where was all this hostility when we were having group sex?"

"Buried under bodies and fluids."

"That was rhetorical," David says.

"Do you mind if Mel and I sleep in the tent?" Amy asks David, who looks dumbfounded. She's surprised his jaw doesn't just unhinge like in a cartoon.

"It's my fucking tent!"

"Oh, come on, David, you can sleep with Jake," Amy says.

"I don't want to sleep with Jake!" David cries, like a petulant toddler.

"David…"

"Oh, Christ, fine. Fine! But only for tonight!" David says. "I didn't set this up for you two to just do what you did already again!"

"You're great, really," Amy says, giving David a peck on the cheek.

"If it rains tonight I'm sticking my body right in between you two lesbian seagulls," David says, mumbling some other swears under his breath Amy does not catch.

In the tent, Melanie smells the sweat of her, of Amy, the girl she loves. And who she now knows, it turns out, loves her. And David's shitty put-down actually does not bother her, for she feels like a bird; maybe not a seagull, mind you, but she has the feeling of being light, of being able to fly if she truly wished. A being in the air, hovering over the flowers and trees, above the people, the cities, the towns. The world.

Her pussy is sore though, in more ways than one. Her vagina hasn't hurt like this since... well, ever. It's not everyday you get triple fucked, then take a knee to the happy hole. And she hasn't had a chance to talk about any of this with Jake yet. Not her sore vagina, but, yeah, the, uh... breaking-up-with-him-hooking-up-with-their-mutual-friend-the-same-day thing. But she can't help herself, she is elated; though also scared, certainly afraid, stigma is surely a factor —what will people say? She's never had to think of herself in this new light. She had thought her identity was more or less set, that the path of her personality was largely plotted. But this? Not just being into a woman, but *loving* a woman, wanting to date a woman.

I mean, how would it even work? Would we get beaten up? Get our shit broken? And what about our parents? Would they disown us? Or just be real awkward, and passive aggressive to us for the rest of our natural born lives?

For tonight, though, lying next to Amy, Melanie just tries to enjoy the pleasant warmth of her body next to hers. And she hopes that somehow, everything will turn out all right. Staring at the half-lidded woman next to her, who smiles in her cute little way, vision sort of swimmy and unfocused, the same as Melanie's; from the tiredness, and drunkenness. Melanie feels everything, and for the first time in a long while all of these feelings and sensations make her happy.

For the first time in a long time everything feels right with the world.

The next morning it is drizzling. Jake is very hungover. The sort of hungover where the body feels pickled. He remembers the night before, but in bits and pieces, like a puzzle he's trying to put together in low light. Jake recalls the orgy—having sex with Amy and Melanie; that at one point in a drunken stumble he accidentally smacked his erect cock against David's, and how they both did a sort of awkward eye catch, then went back to the respective women to keep humping away.

The thing he's having trouble with is why Melanie didn't sleep in the tent with him, and further, of course, why he woke up next to David and his fucking snoring. He's fairly sure David and him didn't fuck (not that he's homophobic, but even if he *was* gay he wouldn't fuck David with another dude's dick).What he's less sure of his why his girlfriend, (who he fears may not keep the title much longer) chose to sleep with Amy. He's scared that maybe Melanie broke up with him last night, but didn't get the chance to tell him yet. It's of no consequence, though. He's suspected they were on the way out for some time now. In fairness, he had slept with Amy. And, well, now he had slept with her a few times *in front of* Melanie, who he also saw getting down with Amy. You didn't need to be a rocket scientist to guess what was happening.

He hears the growling behind him before he gets a good look at the wolf. A black wolf, Jake realizes when he turns around and takes in the wolf in all its lupine glory, white fangs bared. Jake gets ready to grab the closest blunt object to defend himself when the unzipping of a tent close by startles the animal, and it silently slinks off, back to the forest from whence it came.

"You get the fire going yet?" Melanie asks, bed head and squinty eyes to the dawn.

Amy is sleeping inside the tent, and Jake feels the unmistakable pangs of jealousy. The unmistakable sting of hatred.

"Not yet, there was, like, a black wolf."

"A whaaaat?"

"Why… why did you say it like that?"

"'Jaws,' dude," Melanie says.

"Oh… anyway, yeah, big fucking scary wolf."

"Hey, listen, Jake—"

"Don't bother saying it, I know."

A quiet save for the rain as the two of them feel the weight of the truth, though unspoken. A sigh escapes his lips, like the steam valve opened on a boiler. He knows when he says these next words he won't be able to take them back, they will ring through history, his, and hers.

"I got fired, you know," Jake says.

"Oh, Jake. I thought you were getting some help from the government."

"I was."

"You should have said something before we started."

Jake only shrugs.

"It's fine."

"No, it's not fine."

"No, really. It's okay. I have to go talk to some people, or something. When I had the work it was enough, so they started fucking with my assistance checks."

"Well, it's okay, Jake. I can help you straighten things up when all this is over."

"How much longer you think it will take?"

"A few days, most likely."

He steps closer to her.

"I'm a little scared, Mel."

"Aw, Jake," she hugs him. "It'll be okay. It's normal to be scared with the stuff you're going through. I'm sorry for my part in it."

"No, no, I mean... you didn't fall out of love with me on purpose. I guess I'm just, like, unloveable."

"Jake, don't be like that, please," Melanie says.

"Look, I just want to have fun, yeah? We can talk about everything when this is over."

"Jake, you need to talk to someone."

Jake averts his eyes. He hates talking about this shit. He has always *hated* talking about this shit.

"Oh come on. It's been years since they sent me to Iraq."

"That sort of stuff doesn't just go away on its own, Jake."

"Let's just not fucking talk about it, okay?!" Jake says, standing in a huff.

He chucks the white lighter at Melanie, and tells her "you start the fucking fire, I'm going on a god damn walk."

The rain is pissing down, Melanie feels her blue flannel soak through straight to her skin. She does get the fire going, after a hard won struggle. She's never had the heart to tell Jake this, but he was like a totally different man when he got back from Iraq. A new moodiness came back with him. And she knows how not cool it is to think like this, but it's just true, these are just the facts. Jake came back with a confrontational approach he had been slower with before his tour. How do you tell someone you only loved the old them? And besides, she isn't even sure if that's true anymore. *I must have loved him, once. I wouldn't have stuck around for so long otherwise.* But would she have? She was so confused, rushing around looking for whatever job she could find while she tried to figure out what she even wanted to do with her life. She'd never gone to college like her friends, including David and Amy. *I mean it's not like I'm all that old at this point. I'll figure it out eventually* she thinks, and she knows this. The current job she has is at a nursery, and for the time being it suits Melanie fine. It likely won't forever, but they gave her the week off to go on vacation, that was nice of them.

Jesus Christ, where is my mind? she wonders. Even if she hadn't fallen in love with Amy, Melanie had still been trying to figure out the best way to break up with Jake for some time. As Jake said himself it's best not to think about any of this right now, and to just live in the moment. To enjoy the vacation, and the journey. To enjoy the ride.

Amy is next to get out of the tent, stretching, yawning in a cute way that makes Melanie want to kiss her afresh. *Things are moving so fast, though. Is this wise?* Has she thought this all through? It's all so exciting, and terrifying, and exhilarating, and panic-inducing.

What if it's just lust? What if it's a mistake, and we end up hating each other, at each other's throats? What if in a month we're ready to kill each other? What if this ruins our friendship forever? Oh God, what if Amy never wants to speak to me again after this trip?

Melanie tries to remind herself this is all just her nerves. Amy is a good woman, she's known her for many years now. Amy would never hurt her. Amy would absolutely never fucking hurt her.

Right?

Jake gets back from his angry walk an hour later, by which point David is now awake. Jake cooks a late breakfast for them. It's now noon. David seems to be slightly less pissy, but only just, this is what Amy thinks, at least. *Look at him over there, pouting like a child* Amy thinks, followed quickly like *oh that's not fair, how is he supposed to take all of this?*

"So, I think we should take the shrooms in an hour," David says.

"You sure about this?" Melanie asks.

Jake can see the fear on her face. He, admittedly, feels the fear alongside her. Of course he does. He hasn't done hallucinogens in years and years.

"Oh, absolutely! They are great, you're going to love them," David replies.

"You think it's safe?" Jake asks.

"Probably," David says. "What else are we going to do?"

Jake sighs, he can feel the sound and the weariness that echoes with the noise.

"Fuck it, sounds good to me," Jake says, taking a bite of a fried egg sandwich, replicas of which sit on paper plates all around the campfire.

"What's it like?" Melanie asks.

"Oh, shrooms are wonderful," Amy says. "Think like weed but stronger."

"That doesn't sound too bad," Melanie says.

"Mel, we fucking did them senior year," Jake says.

"Well that wasn't, like, that much…" Melanie says, trailing off. "Besides that was a long time ago."

"You're going to love it," David repeats, a gleam in his eye. And David truly means this. He can have no idea of what's in store.

He has no idea the hell that awaits them.

"They will make you puke," Amy says, as she hands Melanie the caps, with a bottle of water.

"You will puke, and then the trip begins. I've given you a smaller dose than the rest of us, since you told me you don't want to see the eyes of God or anything."

Melanie hesitates, staring at the psychedelic mushrooms in her hand.

"It's okay, Mel. I'll be right here. You'll be fine."

Amy gives her a quick hug. With this encouragement, Melanie swallows the mushrooms, and gags a bit at the taste.

"Oh yeah, forgot to tell you, they taste like shit."

"Now you tell me," Melanie says, swallowing the rest of the mushrooms in one rushed gulp.

David, Jake, and Amy swallow their mushrooms, and for a time nothing really happens. Melanie is about to ask if they are working when the nausea begins to hit her; painful waves, that gurgle in the gut; excess saliva in the mouth, she knows the sensations well. She's a puker, Melanie is, she's always been a puker.

Soon the hurling commences, the spewing like fountains of regurgitation; some disgusting performance art exhibit. *Don't wear nice shoes*, she thinks, then pukes even more picturing puking onto nice shoes.

"You seeing anything yet?" David asks.

"Not really, no. Things are just getting a little…"

The landscape around her grows a bit wavy, and unfocused.

"Sort of shimmery," Melanie says, seeing this as she says this, the way the light sort of stretches out in her eyes; the daylight refracting, the colors seeming to take on a different hue, or maybe she's just never noticed them, or sensed them in this way before; Amy is next to her, hugging her, saying something she barely pays attention to, some statements about staying calm, to tell her if she gets scared;

but what is there to be scared of, they are in the woods, they are on an island!; so much beauty around her, and she looks at Amy, and Amy's face slightly shifts, but she is still overwhelmed by this woman's face, by her dimples, her teeth, her eyes, her hair; the smell of her hair, the blonde color seeming to shine with an ethereal glow in the half-cloudy, half-sunny day; the sun vibrant and burning from between the fuzzy white cotton ball clouds. Suddenly the heavens feel simultaneously all too real and completely fake.

Time grows strange for her, the passage of it grows hard for Melanie; indeterminate, not elastic so much as perhaps molasses, sloooowed down, melting around her rather than pouring; and Amy is topless now, her breasts, did they always look like that?; one seems much larger than the other, the nipple swirling a bit, a spiral, the areola like a mini flesh stonehenge, the little peaks and valleys of the flesh as standing stones to be worshipped, a way to gauge the seasons; and what is it summer? Yes, it's summer, Melanie feels the warmth on her face, the drizzling rain has stopped. *A sunny sun on a summer day on a pretty island off of Lake George* and does the sun grow perhaps a little too bright? The sun as a hulking behemoth in the blue carpet sky, rays of heat vibrating; she can sense and now see the vibrations, a pulsing rhythm in the air all around her.

The cat is by her feet. The little grey cat winks at her.

"Did anyone see the cat wink?"

"He did what now?" Jake says. He stands in front of a pine tree, rubbing the bark, staring into the trunk like if he stares long enough some answer he has been desperate for will reveal itself. "Weirdo," she says aloud, then bursts into hysterical laughter.

"Kiss me," Amy is saying, but David pushes her aside to say "kiss me," and Melanie is speaking so weirdly, she says "no way, jagoff," with a sort of Pittsburgh accent, and then she says "wartr," like how people from Pittsburgh say "water," because it sounds funny, and the words feel good from her tongue, forming on her lips, "wartr." *Fucking wartr ice* she thinks, then it's on to, you guessed it, more hysterical laughter.

Melanie does kiss Amy, the cat rubbing against her leg, the feline is now on its hind legs and dancing a bit. "Is that real?" she asks between passionate kisses from Amy; the hawk is in the tree, and the hawk is glaring at her, but the bird of prey makes no move to attack, only sits perched in the hemlock tree, eyes like angry daggers in the afternoon stillness. And does Melanie catch the hawk mumbling "fuck you," under its bird breath?

Amy straddles her on the ground, and Jake quietly says something, and wanders off into the woods; and Melanie half-heartedly says "wait," but David tells them he'll go keep an eye on Jake; so Amy and Melanie grind against each other, and make out. Bodies entwined. Melanie thinks, apropos of nothing *the bees are diseased.*

He's back in the shit, that's how it feels to Jake—the heat unpleasant to him, reminding him of Iraq. He had this friend Stevie in Iraq, this funny guy named Stevie. Stevie died screaming in agony after a car bomb obliterated everything below his waist into roadkill, and if Jake had been just a little further ahead that would have been him; he would have been dying in some nowhere part of the Middle East, with his legs and his cock and balls blasted off, coughing up blood, his intestines like streamers bleeding into the sand. He can see it all so clearly, his friend crying out for help in front of him on the forest floor. He yells, squeezes his eyes shut *this is not fucking real!* "THIS IS NOT FUCKING REAL!" he screams with every part of his soul, feeling like he's on fire, feeling like he is fucking burning. Burning in the heat of the desert. He punches himself in the head, once, hard. "Fuck!" the pain helps him center, if only for a moment.

"Yo, Jake, calm down, man! Slow down!" David calls after him, but Jake is in his own little hell.

The trees seem to hide Iraqi soldiers, black machine barrels like the beaks of birds of the underworld, slick with gun oil. When he manages to dart and look behind each pine, hemlock, and oak there are no soldiers, and most of Jake knows there never were any, this is all in his drug-addled head. Deep in his fucking traumatized, damaged brain.

"I need to sit," Jake says, and he does, collapsing onto the ground, ungracefully.

"Dude, are you chill?" David asks, and David's face now has diamonds for eyes.

"Your eyes are shining," Jake says, as David's mouth opens and snakes slither out, and Jake screams and runs off into the deeper safety of the island's wilderness.

David chases down Jake, who now has teddy bear arms, now. *Fucking weird,* David thinks, until he runs into the witch. She is beautiful, in a dark black cloak, very red lips, blood red lipstick, large dark eyes; they appear black in the shadows of the wilderness.

"You are a pretty one," the witch says, batting her long black eyelashes.

"Why thank you, Miss Witch," David says, following up with "Aw, shit, I'm trying to keep track of my friend, Jake."

"Don't worry about him, honey," the witch says, licking her lips. "You should spend some time with me."

"Well, why not," David says. "You are a very sexy witch, after all."

"Thank you, young man. I do try my best."

"Are you from around here?" David says, chuckling. "Come here often?"

"I come here very often, yes,"

"Why, Mrs. Witch, if I didn't know any better I'd say you were trying to seduce me."

"No need of trying, David. I have the power of nature and the dark ones that dwell within the cracks of the world at my fingertips. I can control the beasts in the field, the birds in the sky. I can manifest my will into the plane of the living."

"That's pretty foxy."

"Isn't it, though?"

"Shit, I really should go help my friend."

"I suppose. I will be watching you, David. If ever you wish to speak with me, just call my name."

"What is your name?"

"Hecate."

"Is that with a 'c,' or a 'k'?"

"Just… go find your friend," the witch says, shooing him off.

David runs off deeper into a copse of trees, calling out Jake's name.

Amy squeezes her nails into Melanie's back as the two of them grind together, messed up out of their minds, having this hallucinatory sex; sensations hitting Amy differently in her new state, the color of Melanie's eyes, brown, seeming Earthly, mystical—powerful. Her red hair seems to float in the air before Amy as she feels the heat of her lover, the seismic shifts in the Earth as the energy of the both of them manipulates the very core of the world.

"Fuck me," Amy says, staring into Melanie's eyes; Melanie, in turn: "I will."

The cat dances by the tent, Amy says "I'll be damned," and then the orgasm obliterates any other thoughts from her mind but the pleasure, exploding in fireworks of light and electricity down her spine, and in the front of her head, like an intense ice cream headache.

Soon enough Melanie is spasming, too. She actually ends up slamming her forehead into Amy's own, and Amy cries out; and the two of them moan, in pleasure and pain, and then they are laughing, so loud and they can't stop; it's hilarious to them now, all of this, the whole situation, smiling and hugging each other; covered in sweat and juices and still tripping hard as anything.

Jake sits on the shore, staring at the waves of Lake George, hearing the faint screams of his tour of duty echoing around him. He tries to focus on the water. At the lapping of the waves. But it's no use. The screaming isn't stopping. Just the wails of dying men all around him on this serene shore, staring at this relatively peaceful lake; light clouds like scattered fog on a sea of sky.

And then the movement among the waves, rippling along, hard to discern but it looks snakelike. Slithering through Lake George like an angry drill searching for drywall. A serpent of the depths, from a cold blue fathomless hell.

He blinks, and the serpentine movement and the creature that made said rippling among the waters has vanished. The screaming has also stopped.

"Hey, jackass!"

It's David behind him. Jake has no idea how much time has passed. Stupid, silly David with his bad jokes; David, the guy who stuck by him when so many others bailed when he got back stateside. People like to talk a good game about staying by your side through thick and thin, but the truth is most people will drop you like a hot rock the second even a modicum of energy is required on their part. Jake's father used to call these people "fair-weather friends," and as it turned out, Jake had quite a lot of those. In fact, as it turned out, most of his fucking friends had been fair-weather friends.

"Man, you scared me. What are you doing?"

David looks so concerned for him. Also, David's face is back to normal, at least, temporarily.

"I'm sorry, Dave. I just… I got caught up in shit, you know?"

"It's okay man, we're on fucking hallucinogens. That's all part of it."

"Fuck man, you're a good dude…"

He starts to tear up. David sits beside him on the sand.

"Shit man, you cryin'?"

"No. Just got some shit in my eyes."

"Oh quit lying, we just were in an orgy together, and I've known you since the 6th grade. I was there when you pissed the bed at Mickey's sleepover, remember?"

"You started a—"

"A water fight, yeah, and I also just let you fuck my girlfriend."

"I don't think you let me do that."

"Look, just indulge me, okay? Just say, 'thank you, David.'"

"Thank you David," Jake says, and he actually means it. Shockingly.

"Who knew I could be sincere?" David says.

"Who knew any of us could? It is the nihilistic '90s, after all. Cynicism is all the rage."

"Well, you're a good friend."

Jake means it. *David is* the *dude. The one dude who stuck around. I'll be forever grateful to him for that.* He thinks about saying this, but he can't seem to bring himself to.

"You're damn right I am. Now come on, let's head back. I could use some water, and maybe we could watch our ex-girlfriends make out."

Jake just sighs, loud and long.

Melanie watches the black wolf, standing by the firepit. The fire itself out now for how long she isn't sure. She should be scared: intellectually Melanie knows this. Yet, she isn't, and she blames this on the drugs. Yet, as if sensing her lack of fear has put the wolf off his game, the animal cocks its head to the side, sizing her up, unsure what to do.

The wolf bows, front forepaw crossing as it dips its chest and snout, then saunters off into the forest again.

"Yeah, nice to see you too, weirdo," she says, at this point to no one.

"Who are you talking to?" Amy asks.

"Your mothafuckin' mama."

"Don't make 'yo mama' jokes, Melanie. Don't make me regret fucking you."

"Can we talk about that?" Melanie asks.
Amy's left eye grows larger as she replies "what's there to talk about?"

How to phrase this, she thinks.

"Where are we going?"

"What do you mean?" Amy asks, snatching a pack of Marlboro Lights from the ground. She lights one with the white lighter, takes a big puff.

"Like, are we a couple?" Melaie asks.

The pause is oh so pregnant. Melanie is terrified.

"I'm not sure yet," Amy says.

"What do you mean you're not sure yet?"

"Just what I said, Mel."

"Can't we just, like, be a couple?"

"This is all happening really fast, Melanie. I barely just broke up with David. And you… I mean, have you even talked to Jake? He's seeming like he's not in a good place, right now."

"I know…"

"You need to go talk to him, Mel. It's sort of cruel just leaving him all messed up and how he is right now."

The hawk is in the tree again. It slides its leg across its throat, as if to say "you're dead."

"Do you see that hawk?"

"What hawk?"

"In the tree."

"Oh. Yeah… there is one."

"Christ, what were we talking about?"

"Go find Jake."

Jake runs into Melanie halfway from the campsite. She runs up to him, and hugs him.

"Oh Jake. I'm glad to see you!"

Jake frowns at her. *Can you really blame him?* Melanie thinks.

"Coulda fooled me," Jake says, brooding.

"Listen, I'm sorry, okay. I know this is rotten timing."

"I had sex with Amy before you, you know."

Now it's Melanie's turn to have her trip turn sour. Jake smiles, and the smiles warps out of true, the sides of his lips going well to his ears. *Oh shit the shrooms are still kicking* Melanie thinks.

"What do you mean?"

"I mean I fucked your girlfriend a month ago."

"She's not my—why?"

"Why not? Do you blame me? You broke up with me on this trip so you could be with her."

"How could you?" Melanie is really hurt, though should she be? It's not like their relationship has been in a good place. Their relationship has been like that milk in the fridge where it's past the expiration date, and you sniff test, and still are never sure even after you take a sip.

"How could I? Quite easily, as it turns out," Jake says.

Melanie grabs a beer out of the cooler, and tosses it at Jake, hitting him in the chest. The beer bursts open, spraying foamy suds in an arc from the ground.

"Oh, real mature, Mel!" Jake says, storming over to her, and she in turn holds her ground.

"I can't believe you cheated!"

"Oh please, you couldn't wait to have sex with Amy!"

"Yes, but there's the whole issue of trust. I got your permission to have sex with her!"

"When did I agree to that?!"

"Well gee, seems to me it was right around the time you started sticking your dick in her in front of me, you tremendous asshole!"

"Shut up, would you! Amy might hear you!"

"She—"

Jake witnesses Melanie realize, about the same time that he realizes Amy is gone from the campsite.

"Where did Amy go?" Melanie says.

Jake has no idea.

Amy stands before the head of the dead deer on the ground, the pentagram drawn in its blood in the dirt; sigils surrounding the pentagram, the number 666, a number Iron Maiden taught her. "Hell, and fire, are soon to be released."

"Fuck you say?" David asks behind her, and Amy just about jumps out of her skin.

"FUCK! DAVID!" Amy grabs her chest, eyes going wide.

"What, what are you so—"

His eyes finally stop at the deer head, and the pentagram of blood.

"Oh."

"Yeah, 'oh.'"

"Should we tell the others?"

"*Should we tell the*—no Dave, let's just keep it a secret, let them be blissfully ignorant to the *fucking satanic animal sacrifice less than a mile from our campsite!*"

"Gross," Melanie says, Jake standing beside her.

Jake is only mildly concerned, but then, less than an hour ago he was hearing his dead soldier friends screaming with all the agony of the damned, so, like, everything's relative.

"Hey, didn't this happen in *Ghoul Mountain Part 7?*" David says.

"Is this the same deer from earlier?"

"No. This one has both its eyes."

"Everyone sees this, right, I'm not just tripping?" Amy asks, but they all nod and say they see it.

"How did someone manage to slaughter a fucking deer without us hearing a single thing?" Jake asks.

"Well, for one, we were all drunk, high, and now we're all high on shrooms."

"Are you guys still seeing shit?" Melanie asks.

"Not really, just the colors and the light is weird still," David says.

"Should we… talk to the park ranger?"

"The what? Amy, look around. Do you see a park ranger?"

"Well, I don't fucking know!"

"Okay, it seems to me we should stick together. Head back to camp, and try to get as much packed as we can, and maybe we end the trip early." Jake nods at his own statement, and has no idea why: blame it on the mushrooms, whatever.

"Aw man, are we really going to let some fuckos drawing satanic shit in deer blood ruin our vacation?" David asks.

"Yes, David," Amy says. "I'm definitely going to let it ruin the trip, and I'd like to get out of here before anyone starts to fuck with us."

"Uh, guys,"Melanie says.

Jake and the rest turn to her.

"We better hurry up," Melanie says, pointing at the sky.

Jake stares in horror at enormous black storm clouds headed in their direction from the mainland.

Melanie desperately tries to break down Jake's tent while he gets the cooler and camping supplies back in, like reusable silverware, and tarps.

"Hurry the fuck up!" Jake yells at her.

"I'm trying!" Melanie yells back.

David breaks down his tent with only a little more success. The problem is most of them are still fairly high, so seemingly simple motor functions are way more complicated than they should be. Melanie's fingers struggle and strain—seem to have the dexterity of those big foam rubber hands they give you at sporting events. Amy is just sort of staring at the sky so Melanie barks at her "start packing stuff up!"

They manage to get all the gear ready to go before it starts raining, but when they get to the shore things go from bad to worse. A pit opens up in Melanie's stomach; a black hole of despair, feeling like she might implode at any second.

The canoes, previously tied to the trees, are gone.

"I don't understand…" David stammers. "Who took the canoes?"

"Well, obviously the same person that left the pentagram, David!" Amy yells.

"Okay, okay, let's just calm down," Jake says. "Do we have anything we could use as a flotation device? Could we try to swim?"

"That was a pretty long trip,"Melanie says.

"The cooler!" David says, clapping his hands together. "We could use the cooler, yeah!"

The first flash of lightning strikes mere seconds after David speaks the words.

"Fuck!" Amy says.

"That's not good," Melanie adds.

"Gee, ya think?" David says, pacing the shore.

"Well maybe it's just some dumb teenagers or something. Maybe we have nothing to worry about," Jake says.

The decapitated body of a deer comes flying through the air out of the treeline, knocking Jake over. He scrambles up with blood staining his green Starter raincoat.

"Ah, what the fuck?!"

"Oh shit…" Amy says, trailing off, staring at the thing among the trees.

Melanie looks back and there is the zombie man with the chainsaw, all rot and menace, revving his chainsaw, doing a little dance.

"RUN!" Melanie screams.

They scramble off down the shore, hearing the chainsaw revving behind them. Melanie darts a glance over her shoulder to see a grin of long teeth and rotted grey gums, yelps, and runs faster. Jake tells her "let's cut into the woods, it'll be harder for him to find us there!" And they run into the treeline, into the wilderness of the island. David and Amy do not follow.

David runs with Amy close behind, the revving of the chainsaw like the death bell, the dinner bell; chainsaw noises merge with the crashing of thunder, the light illuminating with a flash of lightning that hits the mainland; bright flash, blinding, the eye of eternity. Amy is shouting something David can not hear, but David grabs Amy by her arm, and yanks her into the trees, and they run with doom on their heels.

He follows the blonde and the other man, moving with speed, what is left of muscles flexing, fingers twitching, longing for the sound of the blade in the flesh; the feel of the nose of the saw connecting with an arm, or a leg, or a stomach: chain and tiny little barbs eviscerating. Sprays of crimson. Dominating his prey, unsure of the desire why, unsure of why he still moves and functions, but the bloodlust surges in him; surging like a river of damnation, black blood and serpents slithering, the howl of the abyss escaping his lips. The howl stretches out to echo over time, to the night he killed Jamie Lincoln, and her boyfriend Thomas, in 1984. Split her up the middle, crotch to neck; sawed off Thomas' legs as he wailed, then ripped into his trachea with long teeth, roots clearly visible in rotting grey gums, to silence the little brat's whining. Others in the time between. Clara Delter in 1993, he sliced through her spinal cord, then stomped her head to mush, and lapped up the brains. So many others, so much bloody flesh in his teeth, so many eyeballs flying through the air, guts festooned upon his shoulders, flopping arms and fingers, chomping into a freshly severed cock, the boy on the ground gurgling up blood, staring on in a horror so profound it's close to awe.

He is a machine made of spoiled meat; a contraption that stomps about to mechanically separate healthy flesh into spare parts; a butcher of humans. A force of unnature. Two hundred fifteen pounds of rotting violent death.

A monster built only to kill.

"You see him?" Melanie asks, frantically.

"No. But keep it down."

"Sorry," Amy says, quieter.

"Damn it, what are we going to do?"

They hide behind a large oak tree. Amy feels terribly exposed here.

Amy has no earthly idea what to do. *No one tells you what to do if a zombie with a chainsaw comes after you!*

"We watch horror movies, what should we do?" Amy asks.

"I mean, not fucking be here is what we should do!" David says. "We don't have any weapons on us!"

"There's an axe at the camp."

"Yeah, like you just fucking said 'at the camp,' it's not here with us!"

"Keep your voice down," Amy hisses, whispering.

"We could try to swim for it," David says.

"And get electrocuted, yeah asshole, great plan."

"Hey, there's no need for that, bitch."

"Oh what, you don't like it when I call you names? What do you care, we're not even together anymore."

"What does that even matter?" David asks, Amy's eyes going wide as she places her finger to her lips *shhhh. This idiot is going to get us killed with his loud fucking mouth!*

"I should just trip you, and let that monster take you," David says.

"You wouldn't do that."

But as Amy says it, she can't tell if she even believes herself. She doesn't love the gleam in David's eyes.

"Let's just keep going, find a good place to hide. Think about what to do from there," Amy says.

"Damn it, I am still fucking high…" David says, moaning, waving his right hand before his face.

"So am I," Amy mumbles.

"Well this is just wonderful, innit?"

"Where are Jake and Melanie?" Amy asks.

"Oh how the fuck should I know?"

A cracking of a branch close by, and Amy is frozen in place, seeing David stock still reacting to the sound. The little grey cat walks out from a nearby bush.

"Oh you little fucker!" David says.

"She didn't mean it," Amy says.

"I thought it was a he?"

"I think it's a lady cat," Amy says.

"Whatever, let's get going, I don't feel like getting cut in half by a fucking chainsaw!"

David runs off, and Amy follows after, desperate to keep her eyes on him.

Melanie runs next to Jake, the two in step, Jake hazarding glances over his shoulder. Jake trips on a root nearby, and goes ass over tea kettle, scraping his face on the dirt. He scrambles back to his feet, and points at a nearby cave.

"When the fuck was there a cave here?" Melanie asks.

"Don't question it, let's just go in the cave."

Melanie slowly enters the cave, Jake ahead of her. He fishes a flashlight out of the pocket of his jeans.

"Good thinking," Melanie says. "You have that in there on purpose?"

"Yes," Jake says, curtly, clicking the flashlight on, casting its illuminating beam this way and that, lighting up cave walls on the right, and the left. The cave seems to be quite deep, from what Melanie can view.

"How does it feel to fuck a woman as a woman?" Jake asks, apropos of nothing.

"Is this really the time to talk about this?"

"We might die soon, so yeah. Mel. It is."

Melanie has no idea if she even wants to discuss this, but then, he has a point. *Might be dead soon enough anyway. Why the hell not?*

"It's warm," Melanie says. "And there's less razor burn to worry about, less hair scratching your skin."

"You said you liked my stubble!"

"Oh here we go—Jesus Jake we need to keep going, we can talk about this more assuming we don't get fucking sawn in half!"

"What does it matter, without you I might as well be dead."

"Jake… don't say that…"

He turns to her, flashlight beam hitting her eyes, blinding her.

"And what do you want me to say, Mel? That I'm so thrilled with my life? That soon to be unemployed making no money, and then alone, you no longer in my life, that this is all just hunky dory? No. No, I don't want to be alive."

"Dude, don't… I hate when you talk like this…"

"Like what? Like a suicidal Gulf War vet?"

"Look, we will live through this, okay. We're going to be fine, and then we can talk about how to help you."

Then she hears the growl from the darkness of the cave. The bear slowly saunters into the beam of the flashlight.

Beside her, unmoving, Jake says out of the corner of his mouth, "start walking backward slowly, but do not make eye contact with the bear."

They back away, cautiously, slowly. Both stare at their feet, hearing the shambling steps of the bear as its enormous forepaws scrape the ground, kicking up pebbles and dust.

David and Amy find a small A-frame house, red with black trim on two large windows near the door of the structure, making the house look alarmingly like a face with a pointed hat. The front door is open.

"Should we go in?" Amy asks.

David just shrugs, then walks right in. "God damn it," Amy whispers to herself, and follows.

Inside the structure is a roaring fire in a black iron hearth, framed on each side and above by grey stones that connect at odd angles. The stones are not level, like someone simply went out and collected rocks, then started stacking them.

"Hello?" Amy calls out, scanning the room. She takes in taxidermy animals of all sorts, large and small: chipmunks, skunks, wolves, ravens, even a bear at the far end of the house.

"I'm not sure if anyone is in," David says, looking as he speaks, not seeing the woman behind him.

"Is it customary for the youth to simply walk into one's domicile in this modern age?" the witch asks.

She is completely naked, save a crown of red roses, sticks and twigs pointed skyward in the front, which rests upon her dark black hair. Dried mud is painted upon her lithe frame in spirals and other symbols. Upon her eyes is a thickly applied black paint that spikes off down her cheeks, and up her forehead (from what Amy's heard going to a few metal shows it's called corpse paint), and her lipstick is black. She is slightly taller than Amy, though she is barefoot and doesn't have the benefit of any type of height from footwear. Amy is not surprised to learn this woman sends tingling sensations throughout her body, particularly the lower areas.

"I saw you earlier," David says.

"I'm sorry, you what?" Amy says.

"She was on the trail," David says.

"Was she in the nude then as well?"

"Oh, please, shut up and tell me what you are doing in my abode," the witch says, lying upon a claw-footed couch of black leather.

"This fucking zombie is chasing us!" David blurts out.

"Is he now?"

"Yu-huh!"

"A zombie you say?"

"Yes!" Amy says.

"Chasing you around this island?"

"Yeah!" David shouts.

"As in a dead person, walking around with a chainsaw."

Amy is about to speak, then stops.

"We didn't tell you about the chainsaw."

The witch smiles, showing large white teeth, the incisors sharp as a dog's.

"Seems I let that one slip," the witch says, standing, creeping toward them on nimble feet.

"Stay away from me," Amy says, walking backwards, never taking her eyes off of the woman.

"Or what?" The witch asks. "What could you *possibly* do to me. I can reanimate dead flesh, and send it out with purpose, to kill any I wish. I can command the birds in the sky, the beasts in the caves, and the fish in the lake. What could you possibly do to me?"

Amy, having run out of rational ideas, grabs the witch by the hair, and begins to drag her towards the fire.

"OW, WHO PULLS HAIR?!"

Amy drags with all her strength but soon is knocked across the room from an invisible force. David is knocked in the opposite direction. The two fly through the air to crash to the wooden floor.

"My fucking hair, really bitch? You're such an asshole!" the witch shouts, spitting on her face. "I was just going to let my dead man do the work, but now you've really pissed me off."

The witch grabs Amy by the right hand, and lifts her index finger to her lips. Before Amy can brace herself to fight back the witch chomps down onto her pointer finger right down to the knuckle. The pain is thankfully overshadowed by the shock. Amy stares on as the witch swallows her index finger, bones and all, in one large gulp.

"Fuck you…" Amy says, weakly, wobbling to her feet, calling across the room "David, come on, let's go," but David appears transfixed.

"It's no use, dear," the witch says. "I've got my hooks in his mind, now."

David's face is slack, hungry eyes with no recognition behind them. He stands and walks towards the witch; Amy notices he's pitching a tent in his jeans.

She has a decision to make. Does she try to save her now ex-boyfriend from certain doom, or try to save herself? They've had some good times together, sure. But is she willing to die for David?

"I'm sorry David," she says, before running for the door.

Jake and Melanie manage to walk out of the cave without the bear following, but it leaves Jake wondering *well, what the fuck do we do now?*

"Well, what the fuck do we do now?"

"How should I know, Jake."

"I'm out of ideas. Maybe we just go drown ourselves in the lake. Go get electrocuted, hopefully."

"Jesus Christ, Eeyore, let's just keep running."

"Running to where? We're trapped, there's no way off this island!" Jake screams. "We might as well just off ourselves!"

"You know what, be my guest," Melanie says.

She walks off and doesn't look back.

Jake is truly dumbfounded. He's never had anyone just tell him to go ahead and do it. He realizes that, thankfully, at least at this moment, he does not want to die, or kill himself. He decides to go smoke a cigarette.

Amy is in an unfamiliar part of the island, trees blacking out the sky. Her bleeding hand kills, her missing finger already throbbing with phantom pain. She hears the thunder, lightning crashes. The wolf is in the distance.

"Oh not you, get out of here."

The wolf begins its approach, fangs bared. *And why shouldn't he*, she thinks *I'm bleeding like a stuck pig.* She has to find the others. But the wolf follows as she walks backwards, like the witch all over again.

"GO AWAY!"

The wolf does not go away, not that Amy thought it would. She grabs a large tree branch, and swings it at the wolf.

"I will knock your fucking head off!"

The wolf laughs.

"Don't fucking laugh at me!" Amy says, then pauses. "Am I still tripping?"

"A little blood loss, a little tripping," the wolf says, in a low growl.

"Well, I am going," she says. "So, don't follow me, wolf."

"No, you're not," the wolf says.

"Stay away. I'll break your stupid wolf jaw."

"I'd like to see you try," the wolf says.

"I'll do it!" Amy yells.

"Good, then do it," the wolf replies.

"This is going nowhere..." she mumbles to herself.

"Welcome to Camp Nightmare," the wolf says.

"A Stine fan, I see," Amy says.

"No, you are, I'm not really talking," the wolf says, smiling, all canines in the lupine.

"Got them Bumps," Amy says.

"Got that Goose," the wolf says.

"Wow, well, this has been swell and all, but get the fuck out of my face or I'll rip your little wolf nards off," Amy says.

"Fucking bitch," the wolf mumbles, then runs off.

Amy stands alone among the trees, in the rain, wondering where her life went wrong.

Jake smokes a Marlboro Red, sitting on a large, wet stone. He is also wondering what the hell happened to his life. Not just the being chased by a murderous zombie thing; this was, of course, not great. But what happened with any of it? He can barely remember who he was before they shipped him off to the desert.

Was I ever so innocent? So naive? Was there ever a version of me that wasn't torn apart spiritually, that hadn't killed a woman and child, filled them so full of bullet holes they barely looked human afterward?

He remembers back to that day, years ago, in Iraq. Kicking in the door, and shapes out of the corner of his eye. And he had been trained well, to shoot and question later. No one had warned him of the cost. No one had told Jake that after the machine gun fire, after the bullets sprayed and the blood leaked, after the dying tears and the last sigh of air escaped the bodies of the innocents in the wrong place, at the wrong time, no one had told him that after all of this, you carried the dead with you. Everywhere you went the dead were in your brain; sometimes far enough back, hidden enough you could function, you could remember a time before them. Far too often, though, they would float to the surface of the lake of your mind, like an old piece of driftwood.

There was nothing to be done about it, the dead were just a part of his everyday life, now. They'd followed him to work, to the grocery store, to the gym, to the park. A dead mother and child, always there, even if he couldn't see them. Waiting to make their presence known, yet again.

He burnt his fingers on the cigarette as he realized the whole cancer stick had sizzled down to nothing but ash, and filter. He lit a fresh one.

Melanie hides in a bush. Perhaps it is not the best hiding place, but it is a hiding place, nonetheless. *Olly olly oxen free, come out so I can kill you*, she thinks, all too aware that with Jake gone she's more vulnerable than ever.

And what about Amy? Melanie thinks. *Is she even still alive? What will I do if she dies?*

Movement stops her thoughts cold. The rain pours down harder than ever, so she can't see who it is clearly; definitely a person, standing upright, no wolf, or hawk, or bear.

Elated, she realizes the figure is Amy. It takes all her willpower not to shout her friend and lover's name. Instead she opts to make a *pssst* noise. Amy looks like she might faint, then catches her eyes through the storm.

"You almost gave me a fucking stroke," Amy whispers, walking over and hugging her, hard. Melanie lets the embrace warm her. Melanie whispers into her ear "I'll give you a stroke, all right."

"You pervo," Amy says, quietly. "But listen, we need to go find Jake."

"Where's David?"

"Probably fucking some witch."

"I'm sorry, what was that?"

"Let's just go try to find Jake."

Melanie allows Amy to lead her on. To lead her further into the darkness of the island. Rotting flesh stomps on their trail.

David sits on the claw-footed leather couch, the witch gyrating and swaying before him to a music he can't hear. Her body serpentines, hips shimmying, thigh muscles flexing. She still wears the crown of roses and sticks. She is a vision, David can't believe his luck. *I must be dreaming* he thinks, *and I never want this dream to end.*

"Do you like to watch me?"

"Yes," David says, in a state of borderline hypnosis.

He can feel her hold on him, but at the same time, he's not fighting. Amy and him broke up, what does it matter anymore? Why not fool around with a freaky island witch? *Why not enjoy life* he thinks, and if this is the witch pushing him, he doesn't mind.

"Have you ever made love to a witch?" she asks him.

"Does my ex count?"

"Not funny, young man."

"Why do you keep calling me 'young man'?"

"I'm far older than I appear."

"What's your secret?"

"The blood of the innocent."

"I see," David says, though he's mostly just staring at her breasts.

"Do you want to fuck me?"

"Yes, please."

"And what of your girl who was here, this fabled 'ex.'"

"Screw her, she dumped me. And, she's a lesbo now."

"Fair enough," the witch says, unzipping him, and sliding on top to straddle him.

"Awesome," David says, and the witch and him high five.

They find Jake smoking against a tree. Amy spots him first. She *psssts* at him, and Melanie feels like a strange sort of trend setter. Albeit an annoying one.

"Don't pssst at me, I can fucking see you," Jake says, making no effort to quiet his voice.

"What's our plan?" Amy asks.

"I think I might just die," Jake says, taking a long drag on his cigarette.

"This is fucking serious, Jake. We need to figure out some sort of plan," Melanie says.

"Why? Why should I care? I barely want to live anymore."

And here it is out in the open Melanie thinks, *that great big elephant in the room we just try to pretend we can't constantly see.*

"Well I do, and Amy does," Melanie says "So maybe buck the fuck up, and put some of that army training to good use, huh? Instead of fucking standing around feeling sorry for yourself."

Melanie regrets the words as soon as they are out of her mouth.

"Oh, I apologize for deigning to be suicidal around your highness. By all means, let me just not have human emotions, or trauma anymore because it's annoying to you."

"You know that's not what I meant—"

"Oh, isn't it? Isn't that not *exactly* what you fucking meant, Mel? You couldn't wait to drop me like a hot rock the first fucking moment you got!" Jake yells. "I'm damaged fucking goods, I know that! We all know that! So why not let that stupid zombie just saw me in half?!"

"Guys, this is getting us nowhere," Amy says. "So what do we do? Do we try for the water? Do we try for a better hiding spot? What?"

"I'm tired of running," Jake says.

He pulls a .45 caliber handgun from the waistband of his jeans.

"Jesus Christ Jake, did you have a gun this whole time?"

"No. I mean… yes. But not on me. Mel, I take a handgun everywhere, I thought you knew that."

"I most certainly did not know that," Melanie says, horrified.

"Why didn't you tell us you had a gun before?" Amy asks.

"Oh, who can ever keep track of everything. Also, I didn't wan't any of you to worry that I'd blow my head off."

"Let's just go shoot the zombie," Melanie says.

"I'll do my best," Jake says.

"You fired that thing recently?" Melanie asks, not sure what answer she's hoping for.

"Well, thankfully, no."

"Thankfully…" Amy starts, then realizes what he's getting at and finishes with "oh."

"Yeah," he mutters.

"Yeah, it's probably for the best you haven't been shooting it much, you know, like, not into your grey matter and stuff," Melanie says.

"Delicate as ever, my love," Jake says, pressing the magazine release on the pistol, checking the magazine, confirming all the bullets are inside. He clicks the clip back into the bottom of the gun, then pulls the slide to check the chamber is clear. "Killer," he says, then places the pistol back into the waistband of his jeans, resting against his spine. He's never been the type to conceal carry right next to his junk; always seemed to him like an easy way to blow your dick off.

"Let's go find that son of a bitch," Jake says.

"Fuck yeah," Melanie says, throwing her fist into the air.

The witch grinds upon him, wailing out, David thrusting away, staring into her eyes as they go from green, to blue, to black, to red. He finishes inside of her, so hard he nearly knocks the entire couch over; and they stay like that for a while, Jake still inside her, smiling and kissing.

"I'm sorry I have to do this," the witch says.

"Do what?" David says.

That's when he hears the rev of the chainsaw. The blade enters to the left of his neck, sawing through the muscle and bone. Soon the blade has jagged its way through his trachea and larynx, so the only noises made are ragged gurgles of blood as the chainsaw finally hitches its way through the rest of his neck. He watches as his life blood sprays upon the naked chest of the witch, who rubs the blood onto her breasts, and over her cheeks, and forehead. His head falls to the floor, and for a few brief moments he can still see, his brain is still functioning. The witch picks David's head up off the ground, and gives him one last tongue kiss.

Then she tosses the severed head out her front door, and David is still around, tumbling through the air, his head finally landing with a smack on the front porch, coming to a stop.

And then, he is gone.

At least, temporarily.

Jake is at the lead, gun drawn, creeping through the branches and underbrush. He keeps his eyes scanning, looking for the zombie. Waiting for the slightest crack of a dead branch, or sliver of red flannel or blue jean pantleg. The fucker is nowhere to be seen.

"This fucker is nowhere to be seen," Jake says.

"I just saw him," David says.

"David, how did you—"

David's ghost is a blueish white. His throat is severed, head precariously balanced on top of his neck stump.

"WHAT THE FUCK?!"

"Oh… right. Yes. I'm dead."

"I CAN SEE THAT!" Jake yells.

Melanie and Amy just stare in horror. Amy walks up to David's ghost.

"Oh, David. Too soon, man."

"I know, Amy. I know."

"The witch?"

"The witch," he replies, nodding confirmation.

"So the zombie…"

"Sliced off my head, yes," Ghost David says.

"Damn. Sorry, dude."

"Hey, no big. I still got a ghost dick and everything."

"Jesus David…" Amy says, placing her face into her palm.

"You ever had sex with a ghost!" David says, then makes spooky noises "ooowwooooooooooo!"

"Cut it out, dumbass," Jake says.

"Hey, I'm the dead guy. Be nice."

"Okay, well, point stands. What do we do?" Melanie asks.

"I think Jake has the right idea," Ghost David says. "Shoot him through the brain. Haven't you seen *Dawn of the Dead?* Shoot him in the brain!"

"Gee, thanks, Dave. Could never have guessed to shoot a zombie in the brain," Melanie says.

"Well, you asked."

"No, I asked," Melanie says, "And I meant, like, what do we do about the zombie *and* the witch?"

"The witch is very sexy," Ghost David says.

"Yeah, and how does that help us stop her, David?" Amy asks. "Do we find her mortal weakness, a frumpy cardigan?"

"I think she could probably make that work, actually," David says.

"Shut up, David!" Melanie yells. "Like, shut up, if you don't have a plan on how we can get out of here without the rest of us dying, just say so. Otherwise, shut your loud ghost mouth."

"Sorry for existing…" Ghost David mumbles.

And then Jake hears it, the unmistakable sound of a motor.

"Jesus, who is that?"

Forty-three year old Gary Newbridge is feeling good when he attaches his new speedboat to the dock. He ties the boat off and turns to the rest of the men in the boat.

"Okay gentlemen, start your engines!" he screams, pumping his fist into the air.

There's 4 of them: himself, Sammy, Glenn, and the one they all call "Husky," whose real name is Harold, and who has as should be obvious by the name a weight problem.

"Captain, my captain," Husky says, and he cracks open a light beer on the deck.

"Here's to my third divorce!" Sammy yells, then takes a cigar out of his pocket. "Shit, it's raining too hard, can we go find somewhere with some tree cover?"

"Sure thing, fellas," Gary says, putting on a navy bucket hat to go with his golf shirt, golf pant ensemble.

"Glad our bitch wives couldn't make it," Glenn says, and Husky slaps him on the back, and they all laugh uproariously, ah-hahahahaha.

"Let's go drink and insult our wives!" Gary says, perhaps a little too on the nose, but everyone whoops and hollers in agreement.

He watches them get off of the dock, distantly wondering why the others didn't bother to look for the dock. Mostly, he just thinks about having more meat. The big one especially will be a lot of fun for him. Never before has he had such a bounty before him, such plentiful flesh in such a short period of time.

He licks his decaying lips with a rotted grey tongue. He squeezes rotting fits around the grips of the chainsaw. More to kill. More to eat. His hideous grin shines through the dark, rainy day.

The zombie follows closely behind the 4 middle-aged men.

"Hey, who was that waitress with the big ol' hooters you were seeing?" Husky asks Glenn.

"Oh, Tammy," Glenn says.

Husky drinks from a tallboy of Budweiser. He's been pre-gaming all afternoon, at his used car sales job. He's not the best salesman, but he knows the owner; he'd have to do something like stab his boss to get fired.

"She sure had some melons," Husky says, grabbing his own ample bosom and shimmying his fat chest in his hands.

"Ah, this spot is great!" Gary says, throwing down a camping chair.

Sammy and him put the cooler down. Gary has been looking forward to this all week. He can hardly tell, but judging by the time the sun should be setting soon.

Sammy chews on the end of his cigar, then lights it with a butane lighter.

"Who is that pretty young thing you're seeing now?" Glenn asks Gary.

"Oh, Ginger."

"You're wife have any idea yet?" Husky asks.

"Well, I still have my balls intact, so no," Gary says, laughing.

"God damn Gary, how did you swing that?" Sammy asks.

"Met her in the office. She's an intern."

"Up top!" Husky yells, then slaps Gary the aforementioned five.

"How's your bitch wife doing?" Glenn asks Husky.

"Still need a bag to ride her," Husky says, pantomiming putting a bag over his head, and then, of course, he starts dry humping the air, thrusting his hips in such a way his cargo shorts shimmy with the fat around his lower half.

"What would we do without our wives?" Gary asks them all, and they all in unison shout "HAVE FUN!"

Husky is feeling good, fun and fancy free. That is, until the chainsaw connects with his back and works its way through his prodigious stomach. Intestines revved into flying bits of grey-pink meat, and Husky screams as he is lifted by the chainsaw blade, the force of gravity working the saw through his upper torso, cutting through his throat and face, before, blessedly, the chainsaw blade connects with his brain and it's lights out.

Watching from her place in the canopy of the trees, balanced in her black robe upon a hemlock branch, the witch laughs. She bursts into guffaws as she watches the fat man get cut in half. The witch smiles as the rest of his cohorts run off screaming in the illusion of safety to be found back at the boat on the dock. The illusion of safety all humans feel when she and others of her kind knew the truth.

Nothing and nowhere is safe.

"Run, run, you silly little men. There is no escape."

Gary screams "LET'S GET THE FUCK OUT OF HERE!"

But when he and the rest get to the dock, the boat is on fire. He falls to his knees, and raises his arms to the sky.

"NOOOO!" Gary yells to the heavens. "MY BABY!"

Gary falls forward onto his forearms, openly weeping. Things go from bad to worse for Gary when the zombie with the chainsaw, somehow having caught up with them far faster than they had assumed possible, approaches. Gary, on all fours, doesn't have time to get to his feet. The zombie shoves the nose of the whirring chainsaw blade straight into his crotch from behind, and turns his genitals into hamburger meat. The shuddering man barfs up blood and howls. Viscera from bloody scrotum chunks and flaps of eviscerated penis skin fly through the air. If there's any mercy it's that the enormity of the pain is quickly extinguished via a swift slice through his spinal cord, and then the pain is gone, and the pain is merely spiritual, knowing the end is near.

The zombie drops his chainsaw, which skates along the dock, as he rips Gary's head off of his body, spinal cord still attached.

Sammy and Glenn, not wishing to have their intestines, spines, balls, or peni respectively put through a blender of blade run for their lives. The witch watches on, their terror giving her a sick erotic thrill.

She's been at this game for years now. Bending the zombie to her will, killing any who dare visit the island. There's no real motivation, other than the enjoyment she gets from watching.

She flies after them, silently tracking their path to the others. She does her best to stifle a cackle.

Melanie and the rest have had a feast for the ears, sending a terror surging through them like angry animals on stampede. They have yet to see any of the middle-aged men, however. They have only heard the blood-curdling screams; noises of mangling, of bloodletting, of death.

The approaching men wail like their lives depend on it, which they of course likely do. One in piss-soaked khaki pants and a golf jacket runs to where they stand, screaming "THEY'RE DEAD! THEY'RE DEAD!"

"Who's dead?!" Melanie asks.

She hates these weird middle-aged guys already.

"Husky and Gary!" Sammy yells. He's panting, out of breath.

"When did you guys get here?" Ghost David asks, and just noticing their ghost friend, Sammy screams afresh.

"There's a GHOST!" Glenn yells.

"Well, yeah," Melanie says, for at this point it's been 20 minutes, so their dead friend as a ghost is now positively old hat.

"I have a gun," Jake says, determination on his face like Melanie hasn't witnessed on it, ever.

"He'll be here soon," Glenn says, shivering. "He will kill us ALL!"

"Too late for me," says Ghost David. "But you all, hell yeah. He'll skin you alive."

"FUCK!" Sammy yells.

"Fucking quiet!" Melanie urges him, raising her hand to her lips, "shhhh!"

"Oh fuck you, bitch," Sammy says, pointing at her. "I don't need to put up with some mouthy twat right now, my friends just got murdered!"

Melanie can't help herself, and her fist is flying at Sammy's face before she can stop its trajectory. Direct hit with the bridge of Sammy's nose, and there's a crunch as the tiny bones crack. Sammy wails, and falls to the muddy ground, clutching his broken nose.

"You unt!" is what it sounds like when Sammy yells at her, so just for good measure she kicks him in the side of the head, knocking him unconscious.

"Damn Mel, that's cold," Jake says, staring at Sammy's unconscious body, the man's forehead covered in mud from the way his body has fallen.

"No one calls me an 'unt,'" is all she says.

"Let's go find that zombie, already," Jake says, raising the gun, waggling the weapon.

But Glenn is having none of it, and he gets up into Jake's face. Glenn looks very small next to Jake: a chihuahua next to a border collie.

"You gonna let your bitch do that to my friend?"

Jake waits a moment, seeming to mull over his options, then pistol whips Glenn in the side of the jaw. Glenn falls like a sack of potatoes to the mud. Jake bends down to hover over Glenn, who cowers on the ground.

"You call her a bitch again, I'll shoot you in the foot, and watch while that freak cuts you down the middle."

"Oh, I'm the cold one…" Melanie mutters under her breath.

"Oh what, you knocked that fucker out."

"Valid," she says.

Jake turns to the now semi-conscious Glenn, and Sammy, where they rest on the muddy ground.

"Come with us, or don't," Jake says, back in the lead with the handgun. He walks off through the trees. Melanie and Amy follow close behind, Ghost David at the rear. Melanie watches a clear hand shake in front of her face.

"Did you just run your hand through my face?"

"Sorry… just testing," Ghost David says.

"Ghost freak," she says under her breath.

Amy follows Jake with the gun, watching Melanie for some sign of camaraderie. Yet there's nothing, as far as she can tell. Melanie appears lost in the panic Amy also strongly feels. She doesn't know what she was expecting. They are being chased by a maniac. Why should she feel so hurt at being ignored during these moments?

Because you love her, you dummy. But push that aside for now. Now you need to live. You can't have a future together if you don't live through this.

"So, what, you're just going to shoot him in the head?" Ghost David asks.

"That's the plan," Jake says, scowl on his face as he stomps through the rain.

"And what if that doesn't work?"

"Then I guess we'll just fucking die!" Jake yells, throwing his hands in the air, gun still in right hand.

"Maybe we should take a picture," Ghost David says. "'Cuz I won't remember."

"Oh this is not the time for this," Amy says.

"I swear if you weren't already dead…" Jake mumbles, tromping through the mud.

"This etter ork," is what it sounds like Glenn says, broken nose warping his speech.

"Oh, who asked you anyw—"

A chainsaw flies end over end through the air, blade connecting with Glenn's face, impaling him a foot off the ground on a nearby oak tree.

"SHIT!" Amy says, and then they start to run. Jake is still in the lead, all bravado vanished in the sight of a man stuck to a tree by a chainsaw through his face.

Amy watches in horror as Melanie trips over an exposed tree root on the ground, and stumbles.

"Melanie!"

Amy runs over to Melanie, and helps her to her feet. "We have to go!"

Melanie scrambles to her feet, "no shit," she huffs between breaths.

The zombie rips the chainsaw free from the tree, the head all red mush as it slops to the ground. The corpse silently bounds after them. His left eye pops out of its socket, and the creature shoves it back in with one free hand. Jake turns back and pops off a shot at the zombie, the percussion loud right by Amy's ear. There is a ringing, she looks over, watches the bullet enter the shoulder of the zombie, who drops his chainsaw.

"Fuck yeah!" Ghost David says, goes to high five Jake, and his hand goes straight through.

The zombie bends down and picks up the chainsaw with his left hand.

"Crap," Melanie says.

They all proceed to haul ass.

Sheriff Wilson finds the wreck of the boat along the dock, the dead bodies looking like so much tomato pulp from a distance.

"Great jumpin' Jesus, Barry, get a load of this."

"What's that, Sheriff?"

"The… the god damn dead bodies Barry, don't you have eyes?!"

Barry, new to the force this year, finally appears to recognize the red puddles as former human beings, and his eyes go wide.

"Well gee golly jeez, Sheriff. That's doggone awful!"

"Yes, Barry. It most assuredly is."

The sheriff docks the police boat on the opposite side of the destroyed speed boat.

"What you think happened Sheriff Wilson?"

"That is certainly the question, ain't it Barry."

"Yes, it is," Barry says, looking puzzled.

"It… yes, it is," Sheriff Wilson says.

"You bet," Officer Barry says.

"Jesus Christ, Barry, that was rhetorical."

"Sorry, boss, thought it was torical."

The sheriff, feeling like his head will explode if he bothers to answer, merely steps onto the dock to start examining the bodies. Barry steps in a pile of guts, and slips, falls hard in a pile of blood.

"God help me…" Sheriff Wilson says, taking a deep breath.

The witch watches the police arrive with a smirk. The useless local law enforcement has never been a major impediment to her fun. Not for the last twenty some odd years. Unless they've made a miraculous turn around in terms of quality and professionalism, she suspects she'll get plenty of fun in this night.

She came out here in the late 70s. Running from a life she did not understand. People had motivations she'd never understood. Their goals always seemed so small to her. Some menial 9 to 5, to get an influx of paper money to spend on new couches and cars, new dresses and jewelry. None of that has ever interested her. Her desires have always been much grander. Much more devious.

The witch has only ever wanted anything more or less than control over the very fabric of reality. More than worldly desires. The pleasures of the flesh grow tired, though she'll certainly indulge. No, she longs for the power to change the corporeal plane. Like the young man she found on a quiet night by himself in summer of 1979. She watched from the trees as he tried to kill a teenage girl with a large butcher knife. Ultimately the girl bested him, stabbing him through the throat. As the man lay dying, she offered to let him live eternally, as long as she got to gather the souls of his victims. Unable to speak, the dying man nodded his agreement.

And thus, the long trail of blood and lost souls she greedily scooped up like rare mushrooms. Thus, her essence and ability to manipulate the universe multiplied thrice fold.

Thus the trail of dead writ large upon the island, wrought by a rotting hand.

Not bad for a 66 year old.

Fucking headshot, Jake. Headshot! God damn it! He's so angry with himself. In the war Jake had been a decent enough shot. All the bullshit about folding under pressure didn't exactly apply to him. He'd put his life on the line in Iraq over, and over.

Just out of practice, I guess, Jake thinks, already dreading his next attempt to shoot the zombie with the chainsaw.

Except, how much was just not giving a shit if he lived, or died? What does he have waiting for him if they do live? No job, no partner. Few friends.

So it came down to doing this for his friends. The ones he had left. He had to buck up and get the job done for his friends.

"I love you guys," Jake says, as they run.

"Aw, that's sweet," Amy says, through jagged breaths.

"I love you too, Jake," Melanie says.

"You're okay," Ghost David says. He mimics running, though Jake notes he's sort of just floating along.

"Fuck you, too," Jake says, a short bark of a laugh.

"What the fuck happened man?" Sammy asks him, knocking him from his introspection.

"You still alive? Was kinda hoping you died."

"What kind of a crappy shot are you?"

"You're welcome to try," Jake says, miming handing the middle-aged man the gun.

"Well, I didn't say that."

Jake points the gun at Sammy.

"You don't shut up, I'm going to kill you myself."

"Jake, dude, that's not called for!" Ghost David says.

Jake trains the gun on Ghost David, his anger bubbling up over the brim of rationality.

"I'll kill you, too!"

"Dude, I'm already deaaaad?"

"Oh, go to Heaven," Jake says.

"You first?" Ghost David says, shrugging.

"You know what," Jake says. "You guys handle it. I'm done with this. This isn't worth anything to me anymore." He throws the handgun to the ground. "Good luck."

"Jake, wait!" Melanie calls after him, but he doesn't care.

Fuck them all. He'd rather just be fucking dead.

Ghost David stares at them all, the motley crew (*kickstart my heart* he thinks, on reflex) of the slightly overweight man in the khakis stained with mud and urine, Amy in her soaked red flannel, and Mel in her tie-dyed hoodie (*when did she put that on, did she have this on this whole time?*) and him with his weird head that has to balance on his ghost body (he's wearing the jeans and flannel he wore during his murder).

He goes to pick up the gun and finds, not surprisingly, that the gun slips through his translucent blue fingers. For a moment he'd forgotten he was David the pervy ghost.

"Son of a bitch."

"Let me do it!" Sammy says in a huff, snatching the gun from the mud, rubbing mud off of the trigger and grip with his golf jacket. "How god damn hard can it be to shoot a gun!"

From out of nowhere, the whirring of the chainsaw as the zombie darts from the treeline towards Sammy. Sammy points the gun at the zombie murderer, but as he goes to aim at the dead man from hell the zombie taps the gun with the blade, and he accidentally shoots himself through the foot.

"FUCK!" Sammy screams, hopping around on one foot, clutching the foot that took the bullet, and in this position the zombie chainsaw murderer has very easy aim at his leg. The zombie saws through the upper thigh meat of Sammy as he howls and plops to the ground like a child's doll. He screams as the zombie murderer stomps in his chest cavity with one ancient combat boot, stomping and stomping; a wine pressing of the damned.

"Run again!" Amy yells, and they do, leaving Sammy to succumb to a stomping death.

Melanie snatches the muddy gun from the ground as they scramble away off through the wilderness. *Fucking useless motherfuckers!* she thinks, followed quickly by *R.I.P.*

The sheriff scans the island, but that would be too easy, to see the killer in plain sight, somewhere easy they could put him in cuffs. Life is rarely easy, that's something the sheriff has come to accept. *Nothing is ever easy, sure as death, taxes, and that my kid will take the last slice of pizza before I get a chance.*

"Sheriff, who the heck could do something like this?" Barry asks, wiping blood from his face with a hanky. He offers the bloody hanky to the sheriff, who just stares at him, then slowly shakes his head, no.

"I've heard the rumors, but always refused to believe them," the sheriff begins. "Of a man named Lafayette Drunder. We had him on the books on a downright *vicious* assault charge, and we had him locked up. But on a rainy, stormy night like this he managed to kick out the protective screen in the cruiser, kill the driver by breaking his neck, then the car crashed, and he went on the run. We weren't able to find him, understand, Barry? We never found a body. And there were the rumors, sure, but… well who the fuck would believe a dead man came back to life on an island on Lake George and started killing people? Where's the logic? Where would he hide, it's not a huge island, Barry. And yet no one gets a glimpse of him sleeping under a tree, or taking a stroll in 15 years or so? He went missing in 1980, I want to say."

Barry stares on in childlike wonder. It unnerves the sheriff but he continues anyway.

"Yet, we'd get these missing person's cases all the time. And we had no way of knowing what the hell happened, if they were killed here or not, because again, we'd never find any remains. We'd maybe find some blood, but on its own blood, even a decent amount, well that doesn't mean they died, right?"

"But you think it's this man, this man who kills them?"

"I know how it sounds, Barry… but I do believe it now. Yes."

"So you think he caused all this?" Barry motions around him to the piles of bloody bodies.

"Yes," the sheriff says. "I feel it in my bones."

"It is pretty stormy," Barry says.

"No, I feel the truth of the murders—you know what, nevermind."

"You ever heard about that sea monster?" Barry asks.

"Barry, we don't have time to bring up tall tales."

"Well you're talking about a daggum zombie, shoot!"

"Let's call in some back up," the sheriff says, taking out his radio. "Hey, station, come in."

Literal radio silence.

"Dang sheriff, you think the power went out at the station?"

"Would just be my luck," the sheriff says.

"Okay, well, I'm gonna get the barrel," Barry says, making his way back to the boat.

"We have a barrel?"

"Well heck yeah, Sheriff, you can always use a barrel."

"What would I do without you, Barry?"

"Probably get another officer."

"Fuck my life."

Amy screams to the sky, a wordless beastial howl of despair. *We are so screwed!*

"Shit, shit, SHIT!" Melanie yells. "Amy do you know how to shoot a gun?"

"No!"

"Well, fuck! We are FUCKED!"

Melanie kicks a nearby tree, then winces in pain.

"That was stupid, ow."

"Are you okay, Mel?"

Amy starts to move towards her.

"No! I'm not okay! What are we going to do?!"

"I could distract him," Ghost David says.

"I guess…" Melanie says, a puzzled look on her face.

"No, like, I'll do a little dance, and then you guys can shoot him."

"What kind of little dance?" Amy asks.

"I don't know, one with a lot of pelvic gyration."

"This is a bad plan," Melanie says.

"What else have we got?" Ghost David says.

"Maybe we should try to swim for it?" Amy says. "I'd rather get electrocuted than sawed in half."

"Fine, let's just fucking do that," Melanie says.

"Can I come?" Ghost David asks.

"I mean, can you? I don't fucking know," Melanie says.

"I could, like, try to ride on one of your backs?"

"What am I, a fucking whale?" Melanie starts, finishing with "don't say a fucking thing, David."

"You're welcome to try," Amy says. "But come on, let's get to the water already."

They hustle toward the water, can hear the crashing of the waves, Amy can, at least. She looks back at Ghost David. She's spent years with this man, and now he's dead, and all clear and blue, his head is precariously balanced atop a jagged neck stump.

Where do we go from here? Do we have to leave him here? Will he be trapped on this island for the rest of his ghost life? How do the rules on this work?

It's sad for her to think about. She still cares about David, no matter what he did to her in the past. The thought of him being alone on this island for years hurts her heart. She knows it is how it is, but she still can't shake the feelings swirling in a whirlwind inside of her. She wishes things could just go back to the way they were. When he was still alive. The shock of his death hasn't hit her yet; she suspects it hasn't hit any of them yet, least of all David.

They approach the shore, and for the first time Amy notices the boats docked, and also, she notices the dock.

"Is that a police boat?" she asks, to herself, and the others.

"Yes, we're saved!" Melanie cries out.

They run to the police boat. Inside sit two officer missing heads, corpses with neck stumps still spurting.

"Oh for fuck's sake," Melanie says.

Behind them she hears a loud cackling and a Molotov cocktail soars through the air into the boat.

"Might want to run!" the witch cries out, flying through the air, laughing uproariously.

They haul ass off the dock, just in time, as the boat explodes, sending shrapnel through the air. A piece of metal thunks into the meat of Melanie's calf, and she cries out in pain. Ghost David dives from the blast, but this is obviously more from reflex than any real danger.

"Well, fuck me sideways," Amy says from her place on the ground. She stares up and realizes the zombie chainsaw murderer is staring down at her.

"Well, shit."

The chainsaw flies at her face, and she rolls out of the way, the back of her flannel cut off, skin of her back lightly grazed by the buzzing saw. She scrabbles to her feet in the sand, and Ghost David starts to dance off on the other end of the beach.

"Hey! You dickless fuck!" Ghost David yells. "Suck my ghost balls!"

The zombie chainsaw murderer begins to stomp towards Ghost David, giving Amy and Melanie a chance to run to each other. "Do we try to swim for it?" Melanie asks, breathless.

"Fuck, I don't know, Amy."

"Well then if it's up to me let's just do it."

A strike of lightning in the water right off of the shore, the noise loud, like God clapping his hands in their collective faces.

"Oh, screw it, just run for the woods again," Amy says. "And fuck you too, you stupid witch!"

"Are you offering?" the witch asks, laughing and flying back into the trees.

"She is pretty hot," Melanie says.

"Melanie!"

"What?! She is!" Melanie yells.

"Should we, like, kill her?"

"What, the sexy witch?"

"Jesus fucking—yes, the 'sexy witch.' Can we just call her the witch?"

"Fine then, the witch," Melanie says, in her head thinking *the witch that is sexy.*

"Kill her with what?" Melanie asks.

"Oh dang it, do we still have the gun?" Amy asks.

"I'm not continuity supervisor, how the fuck should I know?!" Melanie says.

"Well didn't you have it?!"

"Did I?"

"Did you?!" Amy shouts.

"I don't know," Melanie admits.

"Not fucking helpful Mel!"

"Oh my God, stop bitching, she dropped it on the beach," Ghost David says, handing the gun to Amy.

"David, how did you pick that up?"

"Pick what—"

"Fucking anything, David?! You're dead, so how did you pick it up?!"

"Oh… oh yeah!"

"Well?"

"I dunno."

"Oh my God, guys, we should, uh…"

The zombie murderer is running in their direction with speed. Amy is getting used to running for her life. At least she has a gun this time.

Ghost David runs with them, through the trees, in pursuit of the witch; the woman that probably still has his fluids dripping down her legs *the nasty murdering asshole! How could she kill me?! I'm fucking great, I'm the best! Taken out in my prime!*

"Fuck you, you don't kill me! You don't get to kill me you stupid witchy whore!" he yells.

"You weren't complaining when you were inside me!" the witch calls out from somewhere they can't see.

"David!" Amy cries out, as they run after the sounds of branches breaking in the canopy above them.

"We were broken up!" he pleads.

"Not cool, Ghost David!"

"You can just call me David!"

"You just don't get it!"

"Oh, keep it copacetic."

"You're so pathetic!"

"Oh, and you don't—"

"Look out!" Melanie yells, as a knife flies through the air towards them. Amy dives out of the way just in time, and the knife passes straight through Ghost David, who again from reflex screams and flinches.

"You suck!" Ghost David yells.

A disembodied laughing from the trees. Without warning Melanie is snatched from the forest floor, and flies off through the air in the witch's arms.

Melanie comes to tied to a chair with vines. The witch stands before her, naked now save oak leaves over her nipples.

"Nice look," Melanie says, groggily.

"Thank you, dear. I couldn't help but hear you earlier. Do you really find me attractive?"

"I mean, can't you read minds and shit? You should know."

"Oh no, dear. I'm not psychic! That's loony!"

The witch circles her index finger beside her temple, the international symbol of "that's crazy."

"Well, you're controlling that zombie, aren't you?"

"Yes, and no."

"What the hell does that mean?"

"Just what I said, Melanie."

For the first time Melanie notices the baggy of shrooms in the witch's left hand.

"What are you doing with those?"

"In good time," the witch says, straddling on top of her as she sits on the old wooden chair.

"I think you should stop this," Melanie says.

"Ah, but your pupils tell me otherwise, Mel. They are dilated. That happens to someone in a state of sexual arousal."

"Let me go," Melanie protests, rather weakly. There's a great deal of conflict inside of her, between her head and her body. "We'll just leave, and we won't tell anybody what you did, where you are."

"Oh bullshit," the witch says. "You'll blab to the local constabularies the second you get the breath and opportunity."

"The…"

"Cops, my dear. The fuzz. The pigs. The plodders."

"Ah," Melanie says.

"Anyway, I'm now going to feed you an insane amount of magic mushrooms, open wide."

"Wait, what—"

The witch shoves handful after handful of mushrooms into her mouth. Melanie tries to keep her mouth closed, but the witch pries her mouth open with an ease and surprising strength. Soon enough the bag is empty.

"Enjoy seeing the eyes of the universe, dear."

"I don't want to." A statement of defeat, more than anything.

The witch takes off her jeans.

"Aw, jeez."

"Hush now, dear."

The witch proceeds to pull down her panties, and begins to lick at her; between the drug in her system slowly taking hold, and the horror and pleasure commingled, she is a rollercoaster of moans and terror.

"Stop?" she says, very much as a question, and then her body is made of jello, and her crotch is underwater, and it's like the lightning hitting the lake from earlier, she is all electrical shocks and losing control of her faculties; then she is a pile of water sliding from the chair to the ground.

The witch gets down on the ground with her, and she weakly protests again trying to push the witch away, but the witch has her tongue back inside of her, and she has transmogrified from liquid to meat, like a roast; Melanie is cooking, the juices spilling out of her as the sensations push her past the brink of normalcy. Soon the room explodes in red butterflies, the house is gone and there are nothing but black trees, dark black trees dripping an oil-like substance; black ichor, oozing from the trees as her orgasm turns her tongue to a marshmallow—and she can't really speak english so the words sound from her mouth like "ahfuh," and then the witch's fingers are inside of her and she is no longer aware of anything save the feelings so strong she can't move, think, or even make garbled sounds.

Melanie explodes into thousands of flowers, her breathing is the ground, the rise and fall of her chest mirrors the rise and fall of the dirt on the ground, rising, and falling. And then she gets her voice back, and the room is back, and the fingers are milking her G-spot, and holy shit, holy shit, oh holy shit "I'm!" and she locks up like a seizurous person, her eyes feel like they bug out of her head, her forehead seems to turn into a piece of stone as the power of the orgasm makes her look like a badly marionetted puppet.

And then she is openly weeping, and she isn't really sure why, but then she remembers *oh right, this stupid fucking witch force-fed me a whole bag of shrooms.* And she is still the badly marionetted puppet as she runs from the house, the witch calling after her, who has a third eye in her forehead, a dark red eye, the color of arterial blood; she screams for help but has no idea if it's out loud or not, and she trips on a branch that turns to an anaconda, that tells her in a heavy Brooklyn accent "watch where ya going!"

"Sit and spin," she tells the Brooklyn anaconda, weakly, and she fights through the flapping red butterflies, now back and all around her to *think, think damn it, none of this is real, so think, how do you go get help?!* And she stumbles against a tree, face hitting the bark, but the bark feels nice, rough but nice; she hears Amy call out her name, but how can she be sure if it's truly her, if it's the woman she loves, or the witch, or her own heavily drug-addled mind?

"I'm here, Amy," she calls out weakly, but where *is* here exactly?

At some point night falls like a heavily overweight drunk, crashing into her and the landscape around her, she even says aloud "when is night?" and it's not even a proper sentence, but the fucking vampire next to her won't stop saying "you suck, I suck, we all suck," and she goes "the joke is bad!" but the vampire won't stop, and he looks like one of the Lost Boys, she thinks it's actually Kiefer Sutherland, and she says aloud "you're a real dream boat," and Kiefer from *The Lost Boys* just stops and goes "yeah, no shit," then flies off into the trees.

The bats, the bats wear sunglasses, but they tell her they aren't cool. She has no idea what this means. *Wasn't I trying to do something?* "Yeah, find the others," a shadow says, this shadow is the shape of her, the size of her, and as it speaks she realizes it uses her voice, and has her eyes: blue eyes peering out of an otherwise black shadow, featureless. "How?" she asks, and her words echo and echo among the trees, the shadow responds "do your best," then is just her shadow, not speaking, not with any eyes, just a normal shadow. The bark peels from the trees in strips, like beef jerky, on the other side of the bark it says *eat me* but Melanie refuses, she will not eat bark no matter what writing it has on it. The lemon is floating before her eyes, a cartoon, wide, friendly smile, big old cartoon eyes, singing "call out their names, Mel, call them out!" and so she does: "Hey, Jake!" and she stumbles, and falls, yelling "Amy, come get me!" and then she of course remembers the zombie chainsaw murderer, and decides to stop yelling if she can at all manage.

The trees grow faces, angry, leering countenances; an elm sticks a wooden tongue out at her and blows a raspberry; the sky begins to swirl, purple and white, a soft serve ice cream in the sky; cherries rain down, hitting her hard about the limbs. *Find the others* she thinks, but how will she know if they are really them, and then that fucking song is in her head *how will I know* what is that Whitney? *Oh Jesus, how the hell am I going to find them?* And her right hand tells her *trust your instincts,* but how on Earth can she do that her fucking hand is talking to her?

"Mel?" Amy says, suddenly beside her, and she hugs her, and Melanie says "oh, Amy I missed you," and then Amy says "Well I've been meaning to talk to you, see you're a garbage human and I hate myself for ever touching your terrible body, and I do hope you get brutally murdered," and Mel says "this is really hurtful," and then Amy says "you are a bad person, and Jake trusted you, and you let him down, and now he will probably off himself and it is all your fault."

Amy melts into a puddle of worms, only her face left, deflated on the dirt, as she still speaks "you are a bad and ugly person, I look forward to going to your funeral."

"You're just worms," she tells the pile, and starts to run, running now, her legs becoming robotic, pistoning; she is a machine, an amalgamation, a cyborg, her knees are bionic so she does not tire, she just runs and runs; she wishes her mind was a machine, able to think logically, to extrapolate the pertinent details among the hallucinations and the emotional nonsense barfing all over her perceptions.

And then she is vomiting herself, all golds, greens, and reds, the reds turning into the butterflies, clouding her vision with insectile persistence. She is no longer the cyborg, now her limbs feel like taffy, saltwater taffy left in the sun to pool and melt. And Melanie gives up, it is all too much, everything is simultaneously too bright and too dark; best to just succumb to the elements, and become one with the Earth. *Amy doesn't really love me. She just wanted to get back at David. And now that David is gone, she could give a fuck about me. To her I'm just another pretty thing to play with and discard.*

And poor Jake. He probably will kill himself. The images in her mind, though she shuts her eyes tight: the noose hanging, Jake placing his neck inside, kicking over the chair—his face turning blue, then purple, his eyes bugging out if his head, his legs kicking, then going still. *Oh Jake, this is all my fault! I'm so fucking shellfish!*

"Did you just say shellfish?" the bear asks her.

"Oh shit, I meant *selfish*. SELFISH!"

"Oh, there, there, darlin'. I'm just a bear, I don't judge."

"What should I do, Mr. Bear?"

"I'm actually a lady bear."

"Oh. Well, what should I do, Mrs. Bear?"

"Mel, how should I know? I'm a bear. Alls I care about is eating and then shitting in the woods."

"Fair point."

"But, you could try to accept that you are not the guardian of the world, and that people are responsible for themselves. You could understand that the life and death of a person, largely, they are responsible for that."

"That's sorta harsh, Mrs. Bear."

"That's nature, darlin'. Luck of the draw."

"No, I don't accept your feelings, bear. I will help Jake. He loves me. That makes it partially my responsibility."

"Suit yourself, but that way only ends in heartache."

"Then so fucking be it."

The bear smiles, and pats her lightly on the cheek.

"Things will be okay, darlin'."

From behind her, the voice.

"Don't move Mel, there's a bear right next to you."

The voice is Jake's voice.

Melanie turns to Jake, who has a halo of fire behind his head.

"Well, I know that, silly!"

"No, like, Mel… there's a huge bear right next to you. I need you to slowly, *slowly* crawl towards me."

"Oh, Mrs. Bear is harmless."

"Are you fucking high?"

"Oh, yes. Very. The witch forced me to eat a whole bag of mushrooms."

"Shit."

"Yup. So you say this bear is real?"

"Very real, Mel."

So, being so high she has no real fear anymore, or rather so much fear that everything is terrifying so a bear is the same amount of terrifying as her boyfriend's face, Melanie slowly crawls backwards, not looking at the bear. And then, when she is by Jake's feet, Jake helps her to stand, and they walk backwards, *slowly,* away from the bear and back into the tree line.

Now Jake has Kermit the frog eyes, but otherwise his face is normal.

"We need to find somewhere to chill, where you can wait this out."

"Is there still a zombie chainsaw murderer?"

"Yes."

"Well that sucks donkey balls."

"Very astute, Mel."

"You're a suit."

"No, not a… you know what. nevermind. Let's go find somewhere to hide."

"I love you, Jake."

"You're just fucking high off your head…" Jake mumbles.

"No, Jake. I do. Things got so messy this weekend, but I want you to know, I've loved you for many years. Just because I didn't end up with you doesn't mean I didn't love you."

"You had a funny way of showing it, by leaving me."

"Jake, I never left. We just stopped dating."

"I guess that's true."

"It is! Seriously! How many years have we known each other now?"

"Many."

"And you managed, didn't you?"

"I did my best, you know, after the war and all that."

"Your eyes are made of diamonds."

"Right, let's get you somewhere to sweat this shit out."

Amy walks beside Ghost David. She's terrified that Melanie is getting sawn to bits by some undead maniac.

"I'm terrified Melanie is getting sawn to bits by some undead maniac!"

"We'll find her."

"And how can you be so sure of that? Do you know how big this island is? They didn't exactly give us specifics when we signed up." Amy tries to slow her breathing, she can't manage it. She grabs her pack of Marlboro Lights our of her wet pants, then lights one with the white lighter and a trembling hand.

"We'll find her. I believe that. Her, and Jake," Ghost David says.

"Oh, Jake has made it very clear he wants to do this on his own."

"Come on, Amy. We are doing this partly for him, remember? To help him forget his shit."

"And what does he end up doing?! Fucking wigging his shit again!"

"Oh, Ghost David, so cruel. Still so petty. This is our friend, you dead loser."

"You're the…" he stops his line realizing it makes no sense.

"Yes?"

"Let's keep looking," Ghost David says.

The dead man with the chainsaw follows the one called Melanie, the one called Jake. He has no real issue with these people. They are simply there for him to kill. These people exist for his amusement. They are here for sport. They are like turkeys to him, or deer. Their pain means nothing to him, save for the excitement, which wells up inside; much like the rancid bile that slops out of the enormous gash in his stomach to splash to the mud.

Go forth, whispers the witch's voice in his head. *Be fruitful and petrify.*

And the dead man nods, for he has always done as the witch has asked of him. And gladly so. She gave him a heaven on Earth. An island of death. A place to slaughter endlessly.

He smiles, all rotting teeth and hunger for violence in the darkness.

"You still high?" Jake asks her, and she can see the words, little caterpillars floating through the night air.

"No?"

"How many fingers am I holding up?"

Melanie watches as he lifts his hand, extends 4 fingers, and the fingers grow hands and fingers, and those fingers grow hands and fingers.

"What's four times four again?"

"Okay, so you're still very high."

"No?" Melanie says, not really sure.

"Okay, there's a cave."

"Is that the same one that had the other bear?" Melanie asks.

"Dude, what do I look like, bear patrol?"

"You do have that ranger hat."

Jake rolls his 6 red eyes, and scratches at his horns.

"Don't you roll your demon eyes at me."

"Let's just get in the god damn cave."

Inside Jake pulls a box of matches from out of his neon purple raincoat (*when did he put that on?* she wonders) and finds some sticks and firewood in the cave (*very convenient*, Melanie thinks). Soon enough there's a roaring fire going that only screams at her every minute instead of every 10 seconds.

"Okay, I think I'm cooling down a bit," Melanie says.

"How many fingers?"

This time when Jake holds up 3 fingers, it's only 3 fingers.

"Three."

"Excellent."

"Man, that was fucking crazy," Melanie says.

"She really gave you the rest of the bag?"

"Yup."

"Shit, you're lucky to be alive."

"No diggity."

"No doubt."

"Great now that song is stuck in my head," Melanie says.

"In your head? In your head? Zoooombie?"

"I fucking hate you," Melanie says, laughing.

"Well, you are a Pretty Hate Machine."

"That's... that's not even a song, is it?"

"It's an album," Jake says.

Melanie realizes she is still fairly high when her words echo over and over. And over.

"You ever think we'd be doing something like this?" Jake asks.

"This specifically?" Melanie says, then laughs. Jake laughs too, though she thinks it's probably not as genuine. But what does she know, the fire is screaming at her again.

"Well, you know what I mean," Jake says.

"Jake, I'm just glad you're alive. I'm glad you made it through."

"I guess…"

Colors swirl about Jake's head, cool blues, the hues matching his mental state.

"We're all glad you made it, man."

Now he looks at her, and there are golden colors circling his head, yellows, and warm oranges.

"Thanks."

"Thanks for sticking around."

"I'll stick around," Jake says.

"Day by day, yes."

"It wasn't easy," Jake says.

"Life never is," Melanie says.

"Amen, sister," the red Fraggle says.

"Oh red Fraggle."

"Are you seeing the red Fraggle right now?"

"No…"

"Maybe you should just try to sleep for a while."

Ghost David and Amy are walking, gingerly, with light steps. Listening to every snap of branch, every crunch of dead leaves underfoot. *How long can we last?* Amy thinks, *I feel like we're already on borrowed time as it is. And where the hell are Melanie and Jake? I hope they're okay.*

"You think that fucking chainsaw murderer is close by?"

"I don't know, GD."

"GD?"

"Ghost Da—"

"Oh my God, you can just call me David!"

"Fine, *David.*"

The zombie murderer stands before them in the trees, eyes of great rot in the moonlight rain.

Amy knows it is the end. She does not know exactly how she knows.

The zombie chainsaw murderer rams the blade of the saw into her stomach, and lifts her from the ground. Her body splits in two as the blade does its terrible whir and evisceration.

"AMY!"

Her vision goes grey, then fades to black.

Ghost David looks on horrified as the woman he loved and loves is cut in half, blood and viscera flying. He runs, the zombie chainsaw murderer in pursuit.

"Fuck off! I'm already dead!"

The zombie trips on a dead birch spread across the ground.

"Ha! Eat that, you fuck!"

The zombie throws his chainsaw from the ground with a grunt, and it sails straight through Ghost David to thunk into the dirt in front of him.

"See?! I'm dead, you idiot!"

The zombie murderer makes a garbled cry of frustration.

Ghost David hauls ass off, but not before flipping the zombie the bird. He catches a sight of Amy's dead body on the ground.

David cries out in anguish. "Fuck you!" he says through tears.

The small speedboat cuts through the choppy waves, slicing through the rainy night like a knife through butter. Jasper steers, while Megan, Stephanie, Timmy, and Donald pound beers in the back of the boat. They get to the island sometime around 2 in the morning, and Jasper and Timmy lug the boat onto the shore.

"You said there's, like, a chimney here?" Jasper says.

"Yeah, from an old house that burned down," Stephanie says.

"Right on, dude," Timmy says, finishing a beer, belching, and tossing the empty behind his shoulder.

"Don't litter, dude," Donald says, picking up the empty can, and throwing it into the boat. "A-hole," he mutters under his breath.

"Anybody know what happened with Brian?"

"Who the hell knows with that kid. He's probably watching Salo again."

"How much beer we got?" Donald asks.

Stephanie opens her LL Bean backpack, and Jasper watches as she counts, mouthing the numbers but not saying them aloud.

"Twenty left," she says. She takes a beer out, pops the top. "'Scuse me, nineteen now."

"Well right on let's rock out with our cocks out!" Timmy yells.

"Do you have to?" Megan asks, frowning.

"Yes!" Timmy says, sticking his thumb out of the opened fly of his jeans, wiggling it around.

"Probably even smaller," Stephanie says, and Timmy sneers at her.

"That's not what you said last night!" Timmy says, high-fiving Jasper.

Jasper doesn't even really like Timmy, but Timmy has good weed, so he invites him along most of the time. And Steph is friends with Timmy, and Jasper desperately wants to get into Steph's pants. It's simple friend arithmetic. Add one Timmy, subtract one pair of Stephanie panties, not accounting for a deviation of percentage based on stupid Donald and his stupid tall muscular body, and his likely enormous penis. *Man, Donald sucks*, Jasper thinks.

"Hey Donald, you suck!" Jasper shouts, and they all laugh, being drunk and teenaged.

"You wish I sucked, homo," Donald says, grabbing at his crotch.

"You mom sucks," Jasper says. "Sucks my hog."

"Guys, can we just go get fucking drunk already at this stupid chimney," Megan says, then seems to lighten up and yells "come on!" then runs off into the trees.

Jasper and the rest run after her, laughing.

Ghost David finds Jake in the cave. He's crying.

"Amy is dead!"

Melanie stirs from sleep.

"Did you say Amy is dead?" she asks.

"She is!" Ghost David yells.

Melanie begins to cry. Very quickly she is sobbing.

Jesus Christ, no… not Amy…

"Fuck man, that was so quick," Ghost David says.

"Mel…" Jake starts, hugging her as she weeps. "It'll be okay."

"How the fuck will it be okay?!" Melanie asks, voice raised, echoing in the cave. "I love her and she's fucking dead!"

Melanie collapses into a heap on the ground, face buried in her arms. Large racking sobs warp her body. Ghost David feels so bad for her. He's also sad, but his sorrow is hidden under layers of rage.

"Do you still have the gun?" Jake asks Melanie.

"I don't know," she says from the ground, between heavy sobs. She wipes her eyes on the sleeve of her Stone Temple Pilots t-shirt. "For fuck's sake, when did I even put this on?!"

"The gun is in your pocket, Mel," Ghost David says, motioning with his head to Jake, who removes the hand gun, now back in his capable hand.

"Okay fuck it, enough of this, let me actually go kill this motherfucker," Jake says, pulling back the slide on the pistol.

Donald waves his hands, jumping up and down.

"Guys, I found the chimney!" Donald yells. He gets tinder and newspaper from out of his pocket, begins setting up a fire. It's only drizzling now but it's still cold. He kind of wishes he'd never come out here, but he liks Stephanie. Besides, he's no wuss. Who cares, it's just water.

"How are we going to get a fire going, all the wood is wet?"

"Wish my wood was wet…" Timmy mumbles.

"Grosssss, perv patrol," Stephanie says.

"Eat it," Timmy says.

"You wish," Stephanie says, rolling her eyes at him.

"Eat it," Timmy says, and Stephanie throws mud at him. The mud clumps onto his flannel.

"Bitch," Timmy barks out, wiping the muck off his shirt. "I just got this fucking shirt!"

"Anyway!" Donald says. "I'm using this."

The teenage boy pulls a small bottle of lighter fluid from his pocket.

"Never leave home without it," Donald says.

"Shut the fuck up," Jasper says.

"Yeah, make me, loser," Donald says, looking over and winking at Stephanie, who blushes.

"You guys ever hear the story of the murderer that went missing from around here?" Jasper asks them, apropos of nothing save the environment, the spooky atmosphere.

"Sort of," Megan says, sipping from her beer. "My dad told me about him, once, when he got really, *really* drunk at a 4th of July barbeque. This man killed a few people in the '70s, but he escaped custody, and they never figured out where he went."

"Creepy," Stephanie says.

"For sure," Donald says, but he's not really listening to her, he's ogling her breasts through her now partially wet t-shirt. Stephanie catches him looking. She smiles.

Well all right, Donald thinks.

The witch watches the teenagers from a branch on a nearby tree. The house was from 1910. The witch discovered this by talking with the ghost of one Beatrice Derth, who, in a cruel twist of fate, had died in the fire that took the house. Her husband had absconded with her cousin, and the two had knocked Beatrice out, then lit the house ablaze with her unconscious inside. The witch still talks to Beatrice every now and again.

She can see through the zombie's eyes, and she does right now. Watching the teenagers from his place among the obscurity of the shadows of the trees, wrapped in a cloak of obsidian night. Through desiccated eyes, she feels the bloodlust her man feels. There is still a brain in his head, but the thoughts are simple, animalistic. She watches the mind's eye of her dead man, cracking one of the girl's spines, ripping the tongue out of the tallest of the boys, chewing it like beef jerky. Oh, the grand designs her dead man has.

The chainsaw takes a lot of gas. Thankfully she helps her dead man out. The witch can create gas from thin air, though when she gets the chance she'll rob the odd boat or two. It's always hilarious to see the boat owner's frustration when their prize won't start. How the little losers wave their fists. Always brings her a chuckle.

She is looking through her dead man's eyes, feeling the red hot rage inside of him. The yearning to hurt, and rip, and cut, and eat. He is ravenous. She can't stand to let him wait much longer; it hurts her heart.

Go on, my love. Have your fill.

Stephanie is fucking bored. This island is wet, and boring.

"You guys listen to that Green Day from last year yet?" Donald asks.

"What, Insomniac?"

"Yeah."

"I liked it," Megan says.

"I thought it was just okay," Stephanie says, sipping from her beer.

"Hey… does anyone see that guy standing among the trees?" Jasper asks the group.

Stephanie looks, but can't see anyone. She squints. *Is that a man shape?* she wonders, *or is that just shadows from the trees?*

"I can't see anyone," Stephanie says.

"I thought I saw the bushes move earlier," Jasper says. "But I am sorta high, so who knows."

"Aren't you always high?" Donald asks.

"Well, I mean, yeah."

"Maybe it's the killer from the 70s, and he's like all dead now, and he's just waiting to jump out and rip us apart," Timmy says. "And like, he's got a chainsaw!"

"Oh fuck off, that's so stupid," Megan says.

"What if it's like some gnarly lake monster, and it's waiting to run up and eat us?" Stephanie says.

"That is also fucking stupid," Megan says.

"Well, you're stupid," Stephanie says.

"Suck my tits," Megan says.

"You wish," Stephanie says.

"Ladies, ladies," Jasper says. "You can both suck each other's boobs, and I'll film it."

Megan throws her empty at Jasper's head, it clunks off to land in the mud.

"More fucking littering," David says, exasperated.

"You're sick," Stephanie says.

"I'm not sick, but I'm not well," Jasper says, smiling.

"You dumbass," Stephanie says.

"Who wants to play never have I ever?" Donald asks.

"Oh, me!" Megan yells, jumping up and down.

Stupid bitch, Stephanie thinks.

"Where is this fucking rotting chode?" Jake asks, gun in hand.

"You said chode," Ghost David says, laughing like a moron.

"Look, footprints!" Melanie says, her voice raw from crying. "We got him, let's just follow these."

Melanie wishes she could shoot the bastard herself, but she's never fired a gun before. Even still, she'd like to shoot him right in his rotting zombie dick. And then she'd like to rip it off his fucking rotting body, and shove it down his stupid rotting gullet.

Fucking son of a bitch, I'd like to ram a tree branch up his ass, and drown him. But then, would he even die? He's fucking dead already.

They see smoke in the distance.

"Are there other people here?" Jake asks.

"And are they single?" Ghost David asks. Jake goes to give David a dead arm and his fist passes right through David's bicep.

They all hear the rev of the chainsaw at once.

The witch is seeing from her dead man's eyes as he grabs the boy closest to him with one arm and saws off his legs above the knee with the chainsaw. The witch feels the pleasure her dead man feels as he shoves his fingers into the boy's eye sockets, watching the jelly ooze as the teenager hollers.

Her dead man saws a teenage girl's head off, the head flying through the air; he catches the head, and then takes a big old chomp out of the cheek. She tastes the coppery tang of the blood, the chewy quality of the human flesh. All so very delicious.

Kill them all.

Jasper screams and runs, he's just seen Stephanie get her head cut off! And before that Donald got his damn legs cut off!

Fuck, fuck, fuck.

The zombie with the chainsaw is in pursuit. He runs, and trips on an exposed root.

"Fuck, fuck, fuck," he says, watching the zombie bearing down on him.

A single gunshot punctuates the night air. The zombie turns from him towards the shot. Another shot rings out. This shot Jasper can see: a bullet to the zombie's chest. It knocks the zombie back, but he doesn't fall. The animated corpse runs in the direction of the gunshots, and Jasper takes this chance to run, any thought of the others entirely forgotten.

When he's into the deeper safety of the trees, he hears a woman laughing from above him.

"Who's there?"

The laughter continues. Jasper keeps running. He's way too high for this shit.

"Such a skinny minny," the voice says, and then he is scooped off the ground, held by someone in a black cloak, cowl lowered. The cloaked woman keeps cackling.

He screams for help, but how would they help him even if they wanted to? He's in the damn sky!

The woman lowers her cowl, and he can see her eyes, surrounded by black makeup, the black trailing down in spikes along her pale cheeks. Her lips are in black lipstick. Her eyes are blood red.

"Let me go," Jasper says, not much oomph behind it.

"I don't think I will," the woman says, then licks his face.

"Holy crap, what?"

"I wanted to see how you taste."

"Are you a witch?"

"What do you think?"

"You aren't using a broom."

"And you aren't much of a man but technically you're still considered one, ay?"

"Can you just please, *please* let me go?"

"Oh, where's the fun in that?"

"What are you going to do to me?"

"I haven't decided yet."

"Please don't hurt me."

"Do you have any more weed?"

"What?"

"Don't play coy, young man. The marijuana. Give me some."

"Sure. Yeah."

Jasper fishes through his pocket, and hands the witch a joint. She proceeds to place it into her mouth, clicks her thumb and forefinger together and her thumb has a flame coming from the end. She places her burning thumb to the joint, and singes the thing, taking a big toke. She coughs a bit, and cackles some more.

"Dank nugs," she says, laughing.

"Yo, you smoke?" Jasper says, his fear momentarily forgotten.

"Fool, I'm a witch, we invented using drugs."

They fly off into the rainy night, Jasper praying the witch won't hurt him.

Jake fires the gun, one hit to the zombie's neck. Another shot hits the zombie in the chest.

Fuck! The head, Jake! The brain!

He aims the gun, as the zombie runs toward him, but he can't get a clean shot off. He fires, pinging a tree, missing the dead man's head by inches.

"Shit!"

And then the zombie is revving his chainsaw and swinging it with terrible force, and Jake jumps to the ground, narrowly missing the blade as it slices through the air. He fires off a round from his place in the mud, this one through the dead man's throat, and rancid pus oozes out of the wound right onto Jake's face. He gags and scrambles to his feet.

The dead man gets his chance and saws Jake's right hand off, the gun still gripped in the severed hand as it plops to the mud.

"FUCK!"

Blood shoots from his severed right hand, and he runs; runs in terror from the dead man with the chainsaw. He did his best, but his best wasn't good enough.

They're all doomed.

Melanie watches as yet again Jake leaves her high and dry, but she remembers that back at the campsite there is an axe, one they must have forgotten about in their rush to escape. If she can just get to it in time, maybe she'll have a chance.

The zombie lets out a cry of rage, and then she is running, legs pumping like they never have before in life— running in the direction she thinks the campsite is.

And soon enough she finds it, luck seems to be on her side today. She grabs the axe, and the zombie runs into the campsite, swinging his chainsaw and spinning, howling all the while: a demoniac dirge of the damned.

The zombie swings the chainsaw, and Melanie manages to deflect the blade with the tip of the axe. The chainsaw falls from the zombie's grasp, and this is her moment, so she swings the axe with all her might. Hacking once, and the axe sinks into the rotting flesh of the neck; sinks in like it's sponge cake. And the flesh is already rotting, but the gunshots Jake managed loosen the flesh more still. All it takes is one more good whack and the head is severed from the spinal cord; it falls to the wet ground, rolling and rolling, stopping in the fire pit. The eyes blink, still staring at her, not scared, or even curious. Just angry. Angry like this is some minor set back: like getting stuck in traffic on your way to work, instead of being decapitated.

"Well, go on. Die already."

But the eyes keep blinking. Minutes go by and the head still seems conscious. The head still seems cognizant. And not being sure what the hell else to do, Melanie picks up the head (carefully, as then the corpse head tries to bite her), and throws it from the campsite. And then further having no idea what do to, she decides to go find the tent with the rest of the stuff on the beach. She's fucking exhausted. She could use some sleep.

As she walks, she thinks to herself.

What am I even doing with my life? At my age, and I still don't entirely know what to do for the rest of my days. On this fucking island and Amy is dead, and that really sucks. And David is dead. And yet again, Jake has left me all alone. And he's missing his fucking hand, Jesus.

Maybe she should try to find Jake, but very quickly she thinks *no fuck Jake, he's left me to die a few times now. He can sit and spin, the asshole. This whole thing started for him. We did this for him, and now Amy is dead, and David is dead.*

But it was just like Jake to be so myopic. She knew it couldn't have been easy to deal with all the shit he saw in the Middle East. She doesn't envy him for that. Yet, over the years, he's pulled so much shit, and she knew him way before they started dating. Melanie knew him way before he enlisted, and got shipped off to the desert to die.

Why did I ever even start dating him? Melanie can't remember now. It feels so long ago, like a murky dream of the distant past. She thinks, hard, *come on when did we decide to start dating?*

They went to the movies. That was it. They went and saw some crappy horror movie, and then got dinner after, and for whatever reason (maybe it was the wine, maybe her mood, or his mood) they had kissed at the end of the night. And then soon enough they were making love, and being romantic, and doing all the kitschy couple stuff.

And then even faster she got to see the real Jake. His moodiness. The way he would self-harm, putting cigarettes out on his inner arm where he thought she couldn't see. When she brought it up he'd storm out, go to the bar, come back stinking drunk and start throwing plates, or he would punch a hole in the wall. The time he did that he broke a few fingers. And she would never forget what he said when she asked him if he regretted it: *pain is something I can manage. Pain is what I deserve.*

Christ, was she even walking in the right direction? She should have hit the beach by now if she was, right? She realizes she's a bit turned around. Melanie had been so eager to get the fuck away from the decapitated zombie she hadn't really thought about what direction she was headed.

I can just listen for the water, she thinks. But will she be able to hear the water? It is still raining pretty hard. Melanie has no better plan, so she keeps her ears open, desperate to hear the crash of the waves. She can follow the shore back around to where they'd first brought the canoes in.

Was the canoe still on the beach? She can't remember now. Her memory isn't what it used to be.

I think the canoe is gone. I think it was gone when we ran for the beach, right?

Fuck, she really can't remember now.

God damn could I use a stiff drink. Maybe a whole bottle of rum.

Amy's death is back in her mind. What will she do now that Amy is dead? These feelings are so hard to wrap her head around. *This is what it feels like,* she thinks. *Exactly this.*

And then she hears the waves crashing along the shore, and ahead is the boat dock, so she just has to follow that and she'll come to where they came in, where all their stuff is.

I won't ever get to touch Amy again. Not here. Not in this place. There is an intense sadness. How does one deal with such an absence? Is there any real way to ever deal with such a loss? When you let someone into your heart, and then they are just… gone. No more sweet kisses on the cheek, or dumb conversations on the couch drinking beer. No more of her smile, and her laugh.

And then Melanie wonders, and hates herself for wondering, but she wonders *is it my fault? Could I have helped her if I had found her in time?*

But what could she have done with no weapon? *I could have tried to fucking do something!* But could she have? This was likely all just the grief talking. *Fuck, is there any more beer?* And in the cooler, yes, there is a beer. A Miller Lite, God, what swill, but she drinks it greedily. And then Amy is beside her, but she knows it's not really Amy, because she is glowing gold; an ethereal, bright, warm light coming from her love.

"I know you aren't really there," Melanie says, sipping her beer. "This is from the mushrooms. You are dead."

"I know, Mel. I'm gone. But I can be here with you, for now."

"Well thank you, it's mighty kind of you," Melanie says, crying now.

"Oh, it'll be all right," the glowing golden Amy says.

"How?" Melanie asks, her voice cracking. "You're gone now."

"I'll always be with you, though. You know that."

"No, I know, but like… you are *physically* gone. I'll never get to hold you again, or kiss you. And we were just figuring things out here."

"I know," the glowing Amy says.

And then she is gone, and it's just her, Melanie, sitting on a rainy shore on an island on Lake George. Drinking, barely even happy that she killed a zombie.

They get to the A-frame house. The witch takes Jasper inside. The place is pretty cool, but he's still pretty messed up, and scared.

"Please don't hurt me," Jasper says.

"Oh, I won't dear," the witch says, then blows a powder into his face.

The boy staggers, falls to the floor. His breathing quickens its pace.

"What was that?" Jasper says, crawling over to the couch, dragging himself up and on.

"Oh, a paralytic, dear. You won't feel a thing when I kill you."

Jasper tries to run but he barely makes it out the door before collapsing.

"Sorry honey, but I need a new soldier while I patch up my dead man."

Jasper watches the knife slide into his chest; all he feels is a vague pressure. She's right, no pain, none at all. And it happens so quick, one second he is panicking, watching the blade rush towards his heart, and then—

Megan runs to the beach and finds the woman drinking, by herself. The woman is laughing to no one in particular.

"We have to get out of here!" Megan yells at the woman.

"Yeah, I've thought of that, sweetie," the woman says, laughing, cracking open another beer.

"Well, don't just fucking drink, we need to go!"

"Don't you think I've thought of that, you stupid cow?" the older woman says, scoffing.

"Well, what's the fucking hold up?! We got a boat!"

"Do you?" the woman asks, curious now.

"Yes! It's on the beach! We can just take it and get the fuck out of here!"

"Oh, what's the rush? A bunch of my friends are already dead. So are yours. But I killed that stupid zombie. Hacked his dumbass head off. So why do we need to rush?"

"Because… because a bunch of people are dead and we need to get help!"

"Why? They're dead. Not like we can bring them back."

"But like… we just should!"

"Well, my dumbass ex is somewhere on this island. So, I should probably go find him."

"Well fuck you then, I'm leaving!" Megan yells.

Megan runs off down the beach thinking *God, that lady is crazy!* She finds the boat, and rushes it out to the water, and thankfully the engine still works, though why wouldn't it, they've only been on the island for like, an hour, tops. And then, about a mile from the island, it happens. The boat is flipped from the water, and she's flying through the air, and she has no idea why… until she looks into the water from the air, and screams her last.

Jake is wandering around, barely aware where the hell he is. He no longer cares, honestly. He's lost so much blood. His wrist stump throbs. When the teenager shows up, he doesn't know what the hell to think, or feel.

"You got any painkillers?" he asks the boy.

No response from the teenager.

"Who are you?" he asks the boy.

The boy steps closer. Not moving quickly, or slowly. A normal walk. Still not speaking.

"What do you want?" Jake asks the boy.

The teenager still does not speak. Now that he's closer Jake notices the blood soaking his flannel shirt. He notes the boy's eyes are intense, practically animalistic. A hunger is imbued within the child's sight, the drive written within the muscles of the boy's tensed body.

"Hey man, I don't know what's happened, but you can talk to me. Just tell me what happened."

The boy catches him off guard, running and jumping into the air. The knife now shows from behind the boy's back, in his small, white hand. The blade slams home into the soft spot of Jake's temple. He feels the blade slide into his brain, and then a high pitched whine; his vision begins to grey.

And he is stumbling, and falling. He knows he's dying.

He wanted this, didn't he? He wanted his life to end. So, why is he so scared now? Is it because the choice was taken from him? Isn't this what he's thought about for oh so many years?

Jake falls to his knees. The whining is deafening. He shuts his eyes tight.

Whatever, good fucking riddance. The fear is gone now. *Good*, he thinks. He is glad to die. Glad to have it all end. All the anger. All the pain. All the heartache. Soon to be gone.

Let it end, he thinks.

Fuck it all, are the last words he thinks before collapsing to the mud.

"Wake up, soldier," his sergeant tells him, and Jake is in his fatigues, and he can tell from the heat he's back in Iraq.

"Huh?"

"You deaf, son? Get the fuck up."

He stands, adjusting his helmet, picking up his M16.

"Go kick some ass, son," the sergeant tells him, and he isn't sure how but time passes and he is outside the house. He recognizes the house as soon as he sees the structure. He stands within its shadow.

The house with the mother and son inside.

The mother and son he killed.

"Oh, fuck. No, no, no."

He tries to run in the opposite direction, but a sandstorm hits, obscuring everything, and Jake runs and runs. And after how much time he could not say he ends up right back at the same house.

"*No.*"

He knows what will happen but he can't help himself, he runs again; again the sandstorm hits, again he runs for how long he does not know, and again he ends up right back at the house. With no other apparent choice, Jake steps inside.

"Welcome back," the mother says to him.

"It was an accident," Jake says.

"I know," the mother says.

He is crying now. He can't stop crying.

"I have hated myself since this day. I have wondered why it couldn't have been me instead of you, and your son."

"I know," the mother says. "But these feelings do not change what happened."

Now it's his turn to say "I know."

"What am I supposed to do?" he asks the mother.

"You're in the Bardo," the mother says.

"What the hell is that? Jake says, for he truly has no idea what she means.

"Mommy?" the child says.

Blood leaks from the wounds on his tiny torso.

"I'm sorry. Christ, I'm so sorry."

"And yet my son still has these wounds on his body. And yet I still have my own."

The mother's face erupts in gunshot wounds, blood splashing onto his face, onto his fatigues. He falls to the floor, going into the fetal position. *No, no, no, no.* The boy walks to him, places Jake's face into his tiny hands. The dead child looks him in his eyes.

"We go on," the boy says. "Never in these bodies again, but we go on."

"I'm sorry," Jake says, meekly, in the voice of the terrified.

"We know this," the boy says. "You have said this many times to us."

"I don't know what else to say."

"You have your own journey to make. You need to accept your situation."

"And what is that situation?"

"Do you not remember?" the boy asks him, still bleeding from the wounds on his tiny torso.

And he tries to remember, but Jake can't remember why he is in Iraq, or where he was before this, though it seems important. He is having trouble remembering the last week, the last month, the last 6 months, the last year; time no longer means anything, because he can't remember any of the past few years.

He leaves the house, and the sandstorm hits again, but this time when he exits the storm he is in his civilian clothes, at Amy's apartment. She is kissing him, and he pulls back.

"We shouldn't do this," Jake says.

"And yet we already did," Amy says. They continue to kiss.

And he is confused, but he is also very aroused, and just wants to feel some sort of normal human connection. They make out some more. And he doesn't remember why, but there's a guilt associated with this. But there shouldn't be. Mel and him broke up.

When was that? he thinks. Again, he can't remember.

So they fuck, for it's not "making love," and he remembers back before it wasn't, either. They have a decent enough time, except her face keeps shifting ever so slightly; at one point he swears her eyes go dark red, entirely bloodshot, and at another time in the tryst it seems as though her teeth have grown sharp, like fangs. And then she is biting him on the neck, and it hurts; the pain is overwhelming, so he runs, his neck gushing blood; he feels faint, but still he travels on. Out the door, and the door leads to a place unfamiliar. An apartment.

Who lives here? he wonders.

He goes through the small, dirty kitchen. Dirty dishes in the sink. A lot of empty beer and liquor bottles.

Who lives here?

He walks through the tiny cramped apartment, tiny shitty little TV. Porno mags on the ground, along with old pizza boxes, and other take out boxes. There's a lot of empty pill bottles scattered about; little orange graves in the moonlight that drifts in through the small, dirty window. He realizes his neck has stopped bleeding. Was it ever really bleeding? Did he just imagine that?

He enters the bedroom. He now knows what he will find. His body on the bed is blue. The corpse seems to have been in the bed for days. There's an empty pill bottle, and a bottle of whisky on the bed beside the corpse.

He isn't scared. He should be, certainly, but Jake isn't. This isn't real. He never died from the OD. He called 911 at the last minute, and they pumped his stomach, and he miraculously lived despite all the drugs in his system. And how did he not recognize his own apartment? He lives here, has lived here, *still* lives here.

"What the fuck is this?"

"You're in the Bardo," Melanie says behind him.

He turns to her. She seems unaffected seeing his corpse on the bed. Her face is placid as a still lake.

"What is that?"

"You'll figure it out," Melanie says. She leaves the room. When he follows her out of the bedroom, she is gone.

Unsure where to go, he leaves the front door of the apartment. He ends up right back on the island on Lake George. Ghost David stands before him.

"Oh, damn dude, did you die too?" David asks.

"I guess…"

"Yeah, it sorta sucks, right?"

"Yeah," is all Jake says in reply.

"So you slept with Amy, huh?"

"Yeah. We both did. Earlier."

"No, I mean," and now Ghost David gets up in his face. "You fucked my girl while we were still dating, you prick."

"Now wait a second," Jake says. "You were already cheating on her. What do you care?"

"What do I care?!" David paces back and forth. He's no longer a ghost.

"That wasn't right, dude!" David yells. He has the gun in his hand. He points the gun at Jake.

"What are you doing, man?"

The shot is loud, this is the first thing Jake thinks. This is followed quickly by wondering if he's been shot. He has. The blood blooms through his grey t-shirt. He doesn't remember putting the shirt on. He got this shirt from playing basketball in highschool. It has his name, and number on the front and back. Number 9. He falls to his knees, onto the wet ground. Melanie touches his face.

"Get up," Melanie says.

So, he does. He follows Melanie to the shore. They get into the canoe, and begin to row through the water. The water is still. The rain has stopped. It's a grey day, storm clouds that produce no rain.

"Hey, I think we're going in the wrong direction," Jake says.

"It's the right direction," Melanie says, dispassionately.

The trees are burning. The water is boiling. The sky is dark, and the air is thick with spirits.

"Where are we going?" Jake asks again.

"Many places," is all Melanie replies.

Still on the beach, Melanie (now very drunk, just processing everything that has occurred) wonders what the hell she should even do. "Go get stupid Jake, I guess." *I mean, really though? He is suuuuuch a douche.* And he is, sure, but he's a friend, and he's the only living friend she still has on this fucking island, so she might as well save his bitter ass.

She wanders through the trees, stumbling a little, open beer still in hand. She isn't sure how much time passes before she finds his body, lying dead on the ground.

"Oh, Jake…"

She runs to the body, checks the pulse.

He is gone.

"Shit."

Melanie drinks by the body for a while. All her friends are dead. What now?

And then she hears the branches breaking close by.

"Who is that?"

The teenager steps out from the trees, still covered in Jake's blood. Stains of blood are all around his mouth, like he's been eating cherry pie while very drunk.

"Stay away from me," Melanie says. She has no weapons, she realizes. All she has to defend herself are her fists, and her teeth. Yet, after the days she's had, she's through playing around.

"All right, then. I'm so over all this. Fucking bring it, you creep."

The teenager runs at her, knife in hand. She lifts her hand to block the blade. The knife slices her palm as she cries out in pain. Using her other hand Melanie knocks the blade from the boy's grip. She quickly grabs the knife from the ground and realizes too late she's lifting with her dominant hand. She screams out in agony, wincing as she wills her sliced palm to squeeze around the handle of the knife. She rams the blade into the teenage boy's throat, quickly pulls the knife out and stabs him in the heart. The boy screams a guttural, blood-choked cry, then falls to the mud.

"Good riddance, you scrawny shithead."

Melanie needs to find the witch. Finish this once and for all. *This shit is beyond old*, she thinks. *Playtime is fucking over.*

She places the knife in her pocket, and wanders back to the campsite to get the axe. When she gets there she finds the zombie gone.

"Because of course he's gone," she says to herself, drunkenly picking up the axe, swinging it a few times like a baseball bat.

"This bitch is going down."

Ghost David is bored. He's lost everyone. He can't even remember who is still alive. And he has no idea where the zombie went, or where Jake is, or if his friend is still alive. He wishes he was still alive so he could whack off, or something. He can't even drink, smoke, or jack it as a damn ghost.

"Being a ghost fucking sucks."

"Tell me about it," Ghost Amy says.

"Oh shiiiiiiit!" Ghost David yells.

"Yup, we're both ghosts now."

"It's fucking trippy, right?"

"You got that right."

"You think we could ghost bang?"

"Dude, really? That's your question?"

"I'm just curious!"

"We broke up, anyway."

"Whatever, it probably wouldn't work," Ghost David says, sullenly.

They stand in ghostly repose, and finally he remembers *oh right, we were getting stalked by a killer.*

"You have any idea what happened to Jake, or Melanie, or the zombie?"

"No, I just came back," Ghost Amy says.

"Let's go find that witch, maybe they went to kill her."

"Oh, I bet you'd like to find that witch," Amy says.

"Dude, my dick is a ghost now, could you give it a rest? It's not like I could fuck her again, even if I wanted to."

"Whatever, let's go find this sexy witch."

"Hypocrite…" Ghost David mutters.

The A-frame house is before Melanie. The knife in her jeans, the axe in her hand. Melanie likes the weight of the axe. She likes the feel of the weapon in her hands.

And then the arrow thunks into her left shoulder.

Melanie screams. The witch has a crossbow, and is loading another arrow in.

"You didn't think this would be easy now, did you?"

"Fuck you!" Melanie cries out in pain. "You're gonna regret that."

Before the witch can fire the next crossbow arrow into her, Melanie dives out of the way. She lands hard, the arrow bumps into the ground and she wails in pain. She scrambles to her feet, and runs at the witch with the axe, swinging and driving the blade home into the witch's thigh. The witch cries out, and claws at Melanie with long, red painted nails, but Melanie is too fast for her. She grabs the crossbow the witch has dropped, and loads up an arrow.

"Where is he?"

"Where is who, you dreadful girl?"

"You know who, the god damn zombie."

"I'll never tell," the witch says, pouting.

Melanie bends down so she can get her face real close to the witch. She points the crossbow at her stomach.

"If you don't tell me I'm going to turn your guts into a pinata."

"Now!" the witch yells.

"Huh?"

But it's too late, the headless zombie already has her in his strong, rotting arms. She bucks and tries to break free, but the arms have her, she can't loosen the grip. Melanie can only watch in horror as the witch yanks the axe from her leg, the wound healing as she rips the blade free.

"I'm going to enjoy making you scream," the witch says.

The headless zombie drags her to the fireplace. The zombie grabs her by the hair, and is about to dip her head into the fire when Amy cries from across the room "let go of her, you brainless chunk of wormfood!"

"Amy!"

Ghost Amy stands beside Ghost David in the doorway.

"Oh, and what are you two going to do? You aren't even alive," the witch says.

Ghost Amy throws a log from a stack of firewood by the door, which thunks into the witch's eye.

"Oh you wretched little *whore*!"

"David, get the axe!"

And Ghost David does, grabbing the axe, holding it high above his head, making his way towards the witch.

"Get them!" the witch yells to the headless zombie, but before the headless dead man can move Melanie manages to get free, and pushes him into the fire.

"NO!"

"This is for, well, you fucking know," Ghost David says, swinging the axe hard into the witch's face. The blade cleaves her jaw from her face, the bone poking out.

The witch tries to speak, but can not; it's all the same because the next swing of the axe takes the bottom half of her face clean off. All that's left is a waggling tongue, blood exploding from her missing lower face. The witch falls to the floor, legs bucking, crying out in a strange way one can only do without a mouth to make sounds through. And then, finally, the witch is still.

The zombie burns in the fireplace, and the witch bleeds all over the floor of the cabin.

"YES!" Melanie cries out. "Fuck you both!"

The charred zombie slowly crawls out of the fire.

"Shit," Ghost Amy says.

The lower half of the witch's face gently slides across the floor to reattach to her head.

"Double shit," Ghost Amy says.

The witch bursts from the ground, and places her right hand around Ghost Amy's throat, lifting the spirit from the ground. She throws Ghost Amy through the wall, out of the house. She then kicks Ghost David in his ghost junk. He crumples in a heap on the floor, wincing, muttering "how does that even work?" and then the witch has her eyes set on Melanie.

"Oh, you will feel pain like you've never imagined," the witch says, rubbing her hands together, a gleam in her eyes.

Jake and this Melanie eventually reach land. He suspects this is not the real Melanie, any more than it was the *real* David before, or the *real* Amy. Melanie flatly tells Jake "follow me."

No, Jake is fairly sure this is not Melanie, not *his* Melanie, in any case. He isn't sure if he even cares, to be honest. He's really been through the ringer this last… *How long as it been? An hour? I have no idea*, he thinks, *maybe an hour?*

"Where are you taking me?"

"To the place where all ends, and all begins."

"Could you maybe be a tiny bit more specific?"

"No," this Melanie says.

So on they travel, this Melanie taking point. A lead sky towers before them, oppressive as a skyscraper. The land is mountainous; large dark mountains, such a dark grey as to be almost black. The grasses and shrubs are tinted purple. Jake has no idea why. Melanie is in a robe now, yellow on top, red on the bottom, wrapped about her body: a Buddhist monk's robe.

"I'm dead, yes?"

"Are you?" Melanie asks back.

"Stop answering my questions with questions."

"No."

They reach the foothills of the tallest mountain. He hears singing around him, and is unsurprised to note it is Tibbetan throat singing, and chanting.

"I'm not, like, a Buddhist."

"I know," this thing that looks like Melanie says.

"Well then, like, why am I in the Tibetan afterlife?"

"Why not?"

"Because I'm not a Buddhist!"

"Oh, that doesn't matter," this Melanie says.

They climb the mountain for what feels like many hours. The climb is exhausting, but he doesn't stop, because this Melanie doesn't stop. The trees are all the colors of the visible light spectrum: reds, blues, greens, purples, oranges. The rocks are the same. All becomes a technicolor tableau, hallucinogenic nature. The climb never stops, no matter how tired he gets.

Melanie is tied to the chair, the headless charred zombie to her left, the witch, again completely nude, to her right.

"You're not going to force feed me mushrooms again, are you?"

"Oh no, nothing that fun," the witch says.

Without warning the witch stabs her in the ribs, just below her heart. It's more jarring than anything, so she lets out a pained sort of low pitch yell.

"How old do you think I am?" the witch asks.

"Christ lady, I don't know, 25?"

"Older."

Ah, Jesus, I've been fucking stabbed, Melanie thinks, followed by *this really sucks*.

"Can you just do what you're going to do, I don't want to play 20 Questions."

The witch grabs her left breast, squeezes it, then swiftly cuts off her nipple in one downward slice.

"I LIED! LET'S KEEP DOING 20 QUESTIONS!"

FUUUUUUUU—

"Oh, you seemed to not like that. So why don't I just —"

"MORE FUCKING QUESTIONS!"

"Okay, what do you think happens after we die?" the witch says. Melanie is starting to get woozy, and she doesn't help herself by staring down at her breast that is pouring out blood.

"I don't know."

Ah, Jesus. Ah, Jesus H. Hula-Hooping Christ. Ah, fuck fuck fuck fuck…

"I don't know is not a good answer" the witch says, leaning in, pinching her right nipple, pulling it taut.

"WAIT!"

"Well?"

"I don't know, nothing! Just, like… nothing."

Melanie has never known pain like this. This is the type of pain that drives a person to madness. She'd always figured this could be the case in the abstract, but in experiencing a stabbing and a maiming back to back, Melanie can feel just how tentative her grasp on sanity currently is. She reminds herself about the situation. Maybe it seems more painful than it really is? *Oh bullshit,* she thinks, *I can definitely feel this!*

"And yet you can see your friends have come back here. How do you explain that?"

"You know damn well how we explain that."

"Why don't you tell me what you think will happen to you. Specifically."

"I'll rot in the ground. Worm food. Go back to the Earth. You're a witch, you know how it works."

"Do you want me to take you where we go?"

"I don't know what you mean."

"Well, do you?"

Her nipple hurts like hell. *Or sorry, my lack of nipple hurts like hell, good LORD!*

"You mean kill me?"

"No. I can take you to the place we go. You don't have to die."

"What are the other options?"

"I could cut your clit off."

"Let's go to the death place!"

The witch unties her.

"Oh yes, hold on a second, dear."

The witch picks her left nipple off the ground, and places it back onto her breast, rubs her hand along the wound, and her nipple is attached again. The wound is entirely healed. The witch rubs her hand along her stab wound, and that, too, heals.

"Oh, thank Jesus," Melanie says.

"Thank me, dear child. I have returned thy nipple."

"Thank you."

"I can always cut it off again later, anyway."

"No thank you."

The witch walks to the back of the cabin. "Close your eyes," she says, so Melanie does. When she opens her eyes there is a new door at the back of the house. A black door, which appears to be made of stone. The witch motions for the headless charred zombie to depart.

"Where is David?"

"You'll see," the witch says.

The witch opens the black stone door, and they travel through.

At the top of the mountain is a staircase. The staircase is carved out of the rock, leading up and out into orange and purple clouds. They travel these stairs, Melanie in the lead, up into the colorful clouds. Now she wears a rainbow bikini.

"Why are you wearing that?"

This Melanie stops, and stares at him in the pseudo-blank fashion she has since he first began following her on this journey.

"Don't you like it?"

What a complicated question, he thinks. *Do I like this stand in for my ex-girlfriend wearing sexy swimwear in front of me, knowing she's not really my ex-girlfriend, and also knowing the reason is likely that I'm such a perv I can't even stop thinking about these weird skimpy outfits she ends up in, even in death.*

"I mean, yeah, it's just sorta random."

"I assure you, the clothing is not random," this Melanie says. Is that a smirk he detects on her face? It's so hard to tell with this Melanie.

"Why are you helping me?" he asks.

As if he doesn't actually know. As if he hasn't pieced together yet that this is some sort of shape-shifting angel. As if he isn't aware that he's dead, and this path he travels leads to something new.

"I help you because I do," she says.

"Cryptic as ever, even in a rainbow bikini."

"Soak this in because you're going to be reborn soon."

"My God did you actually just give me a straight answer."

He stares into her eyes, and can not see any joy, or fear, or anything. Just a blank stare you might give to a brick wall.

"I don't want to be reborn," he finally says.

"Oh, stop being a baby. It could be fun."

Oh yeah, easy for you to say. You're some spirit who gets to turn into various people, maybe even various things.

"I don't wanna like, fucking come back as a baby, or some shit."

This Melanie pauses. She turns, facing away from him. He can't help himself, he stares at her butt, because ostensibly this is all in his mind anyway right, so who cares? Sort of a weird flex to have your ex show up in Buddhist robes and then poof she's in a rainbow thong, but none of this makes any god damn sense anyway. He's not religious! He's not even Christian, let alone Buddhist! The last time he'd been in a church was for a young cousin's baptism like, fucking 20 years ago.

And is this a part of everything? Was this meant to happen to me from the beginning?

He thinks back on all the moments in his life, or, at least, the ones he can remember. He thinks of being a child.

Of trips to the beach in the summer, and riding his bike around the small suburban town he grew up in. He remembers going to middle school, being bored out of his mind. He remembers high school, and meeting Melanie for the first time, the *real* Melanie. They met outside school on a Friday while he waited for his mom to pick him up. She'd been wearing a Soundgarden t-shirt, and he asked her about their album (for the life of him he can't remember the title of it right now). And he remembers their friendship, which led to a slow courtship over trips to the mall, hanging out at the food court, trips to the movies, and walks in the forest. Secretive sojourns to drink beer and smoke pot in the woods behind his house.

He remembers the bad times, too. Enlisting, and watching Melanie's face crumple like a broken chair when he broke the news. And the Gulf War itself, the heat of the desert in the Middle East, and the deafening crash of the artillery, bombs exploding, sending fragments of friends and enemy troops alike every which way.

He remembers getting back from the war, having shed blood himself, and the guilt of his transgressions, no matter what justification he had. Coming back to America a changed man, and not for the better. Of the drinking, and the way he'd scream at Melanie for doing basically nothing, hating himself the whole time, unable to stop the hate.

I can't die now. I have so much left to do. There were dreams left unattempted. In secret he'd always wanted to be a singer. To write songs, and stand before a room full of strangers and spill his guts out. Yet, he had not a lick of musical talent. There were a few times he'd attempted to learn on David's acoustic guitar, to no real avail. Even still, the dream didn't die; this dream seemed like it couldn't be killed, like so many other wants and desires he'd had over the years.

And now he was just fucking dead. Or undead. Whatever the hell one was considered in the Bardo. In some state between life, and death. And he never even got to say goodbye to Melanie, or his other friends.

Melanie has electrical tape in X's over her nipples, now, with nothing over her crotch. And he remembers now, the therapist he went to see, the hypnotherapist; he stopped going because his insurance stopped covering it, but it never worked anyway, because he'd try to go to a calm relaxing place (which was a cabin on a lake), and Melanie would just pop up, and be in various weirdly erotic outfits. So then he'd just end up being horny, and it wouldn't really calm him down. He supposes an overactive libido is normal enough, but Jesus, sometimes it felt like he was some sort of freak. He's sure tons of people are just as horned out as him, all the time. But are those people also in a state of limbo? Regardless, now is sort of not the best time to be picturing his ex in basically porn outfits.

He closes his eyes. When he opens them they are at the cabin he pictured in his mind's eye, on a lake. He always pictured this place being somewhere in Maine. There are no neighbors. It's just them. Melanie is giving him a lap dance.

"For fuck's sake."

"The afterlife is weird."

The island is the same, but different. This is what Melanie thinks.

Like the world has been put through some sort of photographic filter, or the lighting has darker gels, she thinks. Everything is a dark blue, the blue that Ghost David and Amy are. It is colder here on this version of the island.

The witch leads the way, still naked. Her skin is still the normal white-ish pink shade. Melanie looks down at her hands, and they are also still white. So, apparently the living stay the same.

"It looks the same but blue," Melanie says.

The witch stops, and turns toward her. She has a crazy smile on her face. A light susurrus can be heard through the pines and oaks. The hints of whispers.

"Keep looking," the witch says.

And this is when she first notices them, in the air. Slowly flying around the island. Spirits. Hundreds of them. Less corporeal than Amy or David, almost looking like mist. The light whispers come from them.

"Where do they all go?"

"I'm not entirely sure," the witch admits. The witch laughs, then sets off to walking again.

"Where are we going?" The island looks the same, and Melanie is more than familiar at this point with its layout.

"I'd like to show you the Void."

It's Melanie's turn to laugh.

"The Void?"

"You'll see," the witch says.

They reach the shore. Melanie stares on in horror, in fascination. The lake leads to an enormous black hole.

"Is that what it looks like?"

"Yes, and no. I don't think it's a true black hole, because we are able to stand here and not have our molecules ripped apart atom by atom. Or something. I don't know, I'm not a scientist."

"How did you get into all this?"

"Honestly? I don't know, it just seemed interesting."

"So no, like, no huge trauma? No one, like, killed your mom who was also a witch and you swore vengeance, or like, no one kicked you out of church for being annoying and you swore vengeance?"

"You seem to be harping on this vengeance angle."

"Well, I don't know! What, you were just like fuck it, time to be a witch? It's witch o'clock, bitches!"

"More or less," the witch says.

"So you're just some horny crunchy lady who felt like taking tons of drugs, being sketchy, and resurrecting dead people."

"When you say it like that it sounds bad."

Melanie stares at the Void, the black hole; noticing the way the spirits travel into and from the yawning darkness. The great black Void before her. Melanie feels so small in its presence.

"This is where we're headed?"

"Afraid so," the witch says.

"To be in this other plane, to travel through that darkness."

"Yes."

"Why bother, then? If this is what I'm staring down, why do anything at all?"

"Oh, shut up and don't question it. You're here, aren't you? This is a privilege."

"I should toss you into that Void."

"Wouldn't work. I can fly, remember?"

"Shit, that's right."

"Besides, you couldn't get me close enough without also going in."

"Guess I'm stuck with you," Melanie says.

"Oh don't be such a bummer. We could have some more fun…"

The witch does a very crude gesture, sticking her index and ring fingers apart to waggle her tongue in between.

"You know, like we could lick each other's—"

"Yeesh. Yeah, I got it."

"I could cut off your nipple again. Watch your fucking tone."

"Oh, I don't even fucking care anymore! This sucks, I'm so fucking over this! I got a god damn black hole *Void* in front of me, and I'm surrounded by ghosts floating through the air like some sort of fog. This is duuuuumb."

"I thought it was pretty cool," the witch mumbles.

"Stuupiiid!"

"Well, fine! Let's go back then! Sorry the gaping maw of the afterlife is such a bore to you!"

The witch snatches Melanie off the ground, and flies back to the door, which she opens with a gesture of her hand. Then they are back in the land of the living, and the witch has a bottle of tequila.

"You want a drink, you ungrateful little harlot?"

"Fuck it, why not."

"That's the spirit, girlie. Fuck the world!"

And the witch cackles, loud and long.

Jake is still at the cabin, but he's managed to get this Melanie to put some clothes on. He needs to think.

"I'm destined to be reborn."

"Sure are."

"As, like, a baby?"

"It could be as an animal, I suppose."

"Oh, that's much more comforting. Thank you for that."

"It's no problem at all," this Melanie says, clearly not understanding sarcasm.

"Can we go somewhere else? This place isn't relaxing me."

"The point is not to be relaxed."

"Well, if we're taking me to get reborn what is the fucking point then? Why walk all this way, why travel to the places we have? Why not get it over and done with?"

"You need to accept your passing."

"Does anyone?"

"Most do. Eventually."

"Does anyone just never accept it?"

"Not that I recall, but for some it can take many, many years."

Jake is suddenly very restless. He's pacing back and forth on the porch of the cabin.

"How long has it been?"

"I do not know," this Melanie says.

He's not sure if he believes her.

"Let's go somewhere else."

He blinks, and before he opens his eyes he feels the heat, and hears the intense churning of something unseen, hears what sounds like rocks crashing against a cliff face. He opens his eyes to see they are on the rim of an active volcano.

"What the FUCK?!"

"You wished to go somewhere different."

"Not to a fucking raging volcano!"

"You all get so picky," this other Melanie says.

"I really don't think this is supposed to happen."

"You all say that."

"No, I mean. I think you've made a mistake. The situation isn't what you think it is."

"Could be a possibility," this other Melanie says.

"Can we go back to the cabin?"

"I thought you didn't like that one."

"I like it better than an active volcano."

"Suit yourself," she says. Jake closes his eyes. When he opens them they are back on the porch of the cabin, the one that may or may not be in Maine, on a lake, though no place he's ever been to draw from.

"I don't suppose you have a boss you could talk to or anything."

"In a way."

"In what way?"

"I can straighten this out."

"Can you, though? You seem sort of not in control of things, necessarily."

"To the ant the bird is unknowable."

"I liked you better naked. At least then all this crazy bullshit was easier to take."

And then, of course, this other Melanie is naked again.

"Well, now this just feels exploitative."

Melanie and the witch drink, but out of the corner of her eye she notices her ghost friends have snuck back in. The headless zombie has not seen them yet—which of course is insane because how is he seeing anyway? *Honestly, how the fuck does that even work?*

"Where's that fucker's head?" Melanie asks.

"Oh, I don't remember. I think it's in a cabinet somewhere. Didn't want to lose it."

"So you put it into a cabinet to not lose it… but you forgot which cabinet, and lost it."

"I do my best, dear."

Melanie begins to form the plot in her mind. And she hopes the witch is too drunk, or too trying-to-get-in-her-pants to be very perceptive. She has no way to tell her ghost friends the plan, so she settles for sort of motioning with her head for them to come in. She mimes stabbing someone with her hand out of the witch's view. They nod in acquiescence.

"Let's fool around," Melanie says.

The witch makes out with her, hungrily, greedily, practically sucking Melanie's tongue out of her mouth. And then Ghost Amy and Ghost David manage to grab both her arms. Before the witch can register what's going on Melanie has retrieved the axe from the ground and hacks off her head in one, two, three hacks. Then she screams at Ghost David to go toss the head into the lake. Ghost David grabs the witch's still screaming and cursing head, and flies off. Ghost Amy holds onto the bucking headless corpse of the witch as the thing tries to escape. Melanie hacks off the arms, then the legs.

"Go to the opposite end of the island and toss the arms in the lake! I'm going to bury the legs. GO!"

Melanie runs away from the witch's A frame house and finds a spot a half mile off. She digs with her hands. She yells and grunts with the exertion, getting a whole deep enough; she manages only about a foot, and throws the legs in. For good measure she jumps in the hole, relishing the cracking bones she hears as she literally dances on the witch's grave. Well, *one of* the witch's graves.

Ghost Amy and David come back, and explain they did what they were asked.

"So how long you think it'll take for her to come back?"

"I don't know. Maybe this was enough," Melanie says.

"We'll probably be gone by the time she's back together, even if she can manage that," Ghost David says.

"Has anyone seen Jake come back as a ghost?"

Her two ghost friends shake their ghost heads in the negative.

"I hope he's doing all right," Melanie says.

She and the rest wander away from the A frame cabin. Melanie remembers "hey, where did the zombie go?"

"No idea," ghost Amy says.

"Should we make sure he's dead?"

"Oh, I'm sure it'll be fine. Isn't it always?" Ghost David says, laughing.

"Yeah. Whatever, let's try to get the fuck out of here," Melanie says.

He whispers his secret to her.

"Oh."

"Yeah."

"Oh, well this changes things."

"I figured it would."

"Mistakes do happen," this Melanie says.

"So are you an angel, or something?"

"Or something."

"So is it, like, crazy sketchy if I wanted to get busy with you?"

"You would wish to do this?" this Melanie says.

"I mean, I guess I'm dead so my morals are pretty much all fucked up."

This Melanie seems to think about the proposition.

"I suppose," this Melanie says.

"You sure?"

This Melanie stares at him, blankly. He assumes she's still thinking. But Jake has no real idea.

"Sure. Why the heck not. Haven't done this in ages," this Melanie, or whoever she is, says.

"Can we, like, do it in the clouds?"

"Dude."

"What? I'll probably never get the chance to be able to again!"

"I am basically a product of your mind, it would be like masturbating in the clouds."

"As if that is going to stop me."

"Eh, fair enough."

He closes his eyes. This Melanie rests on a cloud.

Everything is all he expected, and more. When they are done he dresses on the cloud, and asks this Melanie "uh, was it, like, good for you?"

"Yes," this Melanie says, affectless.

"Man, it would really help my self-esteem on this if you had, like, any emotions you conveyed."

"I did enjoy myself. Truly."

"Well, good. What happens now? Also, that wasn't like, weird of me, right?"

"Yes."

"Yes it was weird?"

"Yes."

"But you enjoyed yourself."

"Yes."

"I... okay, nevermind. How do I get out of here?"

"You have about 30 minutes left."

"Until I can go back?"

"Yes."

"Well, so what do we do until then?"

This Melanie sits on the cloud in the lotus position, closing her eyes.

"Ah, yes. Sit in silence. Got it."

Back to where it all started, though technically things had started at the gas station; Melanie stands beside her now dead friends. Ghost David and Ghost Amy. A lot has happened on this trip, as indeed she expected. Getting together with Amy, and Jake, and David along for the ride. And she almost feels bad, but then she remembers, and it was nobody's fault, really. The heart just wants what it wants.

There are still grey storm clouds, but it has stopped raining. Her smile is natural, though she feels a sadness.

"How much longer, you think?" Ghost David asks.

"Who knows," Melanie says.

"The shadow knows," Ghost Amy says.

"Oh my God, if you weren't dead already," Melanie says.

"Do you think Jake will be back soon?" Amy asks.

"I don't know," Melanie replies.

"I can't wait to see him again," David says.

"Same," Amy says.

"This whole thing has been a trip and a half," Amy says.

"Right?" David says.

"It makes you question everything," Melanie says. "Like, what even is reality anymore? What is perception? Is it just what your eyes see, what your brain processes? In that case reality is completely malleable. If reality is just what you see, and hear, and feel, and if that can be created for you, then what is reality? Reality changes depending upon the situation."

"Amen to that," David says.

"Wait, when did that boat get here?" Melanie asks.

On the shore the canoe is back. Then she hears the chainsaw behind them.

"Oh, for fuck's sake."

The headless, charred zombie with the chainsaw runs at them, though Melanie still has no fucking idea how he knows where to go. Maybe it's like a snake, with vibrations or something.

For the first time she notices what is next to the boat.

"You gotta be fucking kidding me."

There's a chainsaw.

"Oh shit, chainsaw fight!" David yells.

"Fuck it," Melanie says.

She lifts the chainsaw from the sand, and revs it up. Feels the power of the revving blade in her hands; feels the strain in her arms hefting the thing. Melanie runs at the zombie with the chainsaw, her own chainsaw raised. The two blades spark together, and the zombie overpowers her, his blade just barely slicing into her thigh.

"Shit!"

Blood gushing from the flesh wound.

"How dare you make me bleed blood!"

She cuts off the zombie's arm holding the chainsaw. The arm, chainsaw still in hand, plops to the ground. The chainsaw begins to skate towards her across the sand, hand and arm still attached.

"*Shit, shit, shit.*"

The headless burnt zombie runs up and snatches the chainsaw from the ground with his remaining hand. He seems to have no trouble operating the blade left-handed.

"I don't know who you were in life, and I don't care. You killed my friends. So fuck you."

Melanie dives through the air with her chainsaw, and slices the zombie's other arm off. She hits the ground hard, chainsaw digging into the ground. Then she rights herself, stands, and cuts off the zombie's legs with one swift swoosh. The zombie's torso crashes to the ground.

She stands over the zombie. This dead man that has caused her so much pain, mental, and physical. She lifts the chainsaw above her head.

"Rot in pieces."

Then she brings the blade down onto his head, sawing through his brain and face, going further to slice down his torso, ending at his zombie junk. Guts and bits of dead genitalia and other organs, grey-blue brain matter flying into the air like streamers at a party for the damned.

She spits on him for good measure, then stomps the remainder of his head into pulp.

"And now, please, just FUCKING STAY DEAD."

"Fuck yeah!" Amy yells, and David joins in with "Rot in hell you dead dickhead!"

"Now, can we please, *please* get the fuck out of here."

"Sure thing, Mel," David says.

"She gets into the boat."

Amy and David stay on the shore.

"Come on, guys. Let's go."

"We can't," Amy says.

"What?"

"We have to stay here," David says.

"Fuck… no."

"I'm sorry," Amy tells her.

Melanie walks over and kisses Amy. She can feel cold, like a cold wind somehow has formed into a person. A tear streams down her cheek.

"I'll come back," Melanie says.

"I know you will," Amy says.

"Okay. Get out of here, Melanie," Amy says.

"Okay." Melanie sheds a few more silent tears.

She gets into the wobbly boat, nearly falling into the water. But she manages to right herself, and sit. Melanie paddles away, staring at the ghosts of her dead friends waiting on the shore.

Out on Lake George, and now the island is just barely visible through a light fog that has formed. Something bumps the boat.

"The fuck was that?"

Another bump, this one almost knocking her out of the boat.

Was it the zombie? But what kind of sense did that make, he was cut into pieces. The witch? Maybe, but same, and why would she attack her from the water?

Another great jolt, and this time she is knocked out of the canoe. Melanie flies through the air. She lands in the water.

And then she sees the thing. Her blood goes cold.

Long and serpentine. She can't see the head, but it looks to be 30 feet in length if it's a foot, long rippling serpent body slithering with ease through the lake. The head leaves the surface of the lake and it is a huge, somehow dog-like, aqua green, and the teeth are gigantic, the size of her hands, long and serrated.

She swims as fast as she can but there's no outswimming this monster. The thing bites onto her legs, and drags her under the water.

She descends into Lake George, watching the light from the surface slowly fade. The creature lets go and swims back around, and launches towards her, opening its jaws, and she knows with one great bite it will split her upper torso and swallow her whole.

Melanie closes her eyes and waits for the killing strike.

A 67-year-old Melanie sits up, and yanks the headset off.

"A sea monster?! God, what a stupid twist ending."

A 65-year-old Amy rushes over, and gives her a great big hug.

"You're back!"

"Is David out?"

"Right here," a 67-year-old David says.

"What about Jake?" Melanie asks.

"He's not back yet," David says, concern in his voice.

"Is that normal?" Melanie asks the tech at the control board, in front of monitors showing the virtual island on Lake George they just spent real time days on. At least she thinks it was real time days: it might not have been minute to minute accurate.

"Oh, it can happen," the tech says. He's in his thirties, bald, with a white lab coat; above the right breast pocket a badge says William, and the company name underneath "VR Experience."

69-year-old Jake lies on the padded chair, which resembles furniture from a doctor's office. His headset is on, wires leading from the headgear down the chair, snaking along to holes in the floor, which work under the floor to connect to terminals and screens the tech sits behind.

"Do you see him anywhere in there?" Melanie asks.

"No," the VR tech says, looking at various feeds, cycling through different camera angles.

"What's going on?" Amy asks.

"Nothing, Jake isn't back yet," Melanie says.

"Well, where is he?" David asks.

"I don't know," the tech admits.

Melanie hears Jake gasp across the room, and hears him scrambling to take off his headset. She runs over as fast as her older body will allow, and places hands onto his shoulders. "It's okay Jake, you're back! It's all right!"

"Dude, what the fuck was that?" Jake says, groggy. He stands, and makes his way on shaky legs over to the tech. "The fucking Bardo shit. That was messed up, why would you program that in?"

"What… what are you talking about?" the tech asks.

A pregnant silence fills the room. Melanie, like the rest, has no idea what Jake is talking about.

"The fucking shit with my friends as stand-ins you programmed, and the volcano, and the cabin, and all the weirdly specific shit you managed to pull from my head and program into this VR bullshit."

"We didn't do anything like that," the tech says. "We programmed in the trip to Lake George you all told us about from 1996, and we programmed in certain shroom trip hallucinations. You know, the talking cat, and the other weirdness. But we didn't plug in this… are you talking about the like, Buddhist afterlife? As in *that* Bardo? The state between death and rebirth?"

"Yes. That's exactly what I'm talking about."

"Man, we didn't do anything like that."

"Well… wait, what?"

"Look, I'll look through the compiled footage we have for the tape we make you. But I'm telling you, according to the visual feeds you died, and then you came back here, and that was it. We have no record of anything occurring after you died in the simulation."

"Just look into it, I don't fucking now, maybe I had a damn stroke," 69-year-old Jake says.

"I mean, we monitor your levels the whole experience, and it never really seemed like you had any kind of health issues."

"Just fucking look into it!" Jake yells, and Melanie rubs his shoulder. "Hey, calm down Jake. Maybe it was just a nightmare. That can happen right?" she asks the tech.

"Yes, of course it can. It's not common, but there's still a lot we don't know about how the brain processes our virtual technology. There's a chance some minor type of programming error occurred and you ended up falling asleep, and had a bad nightmare."

"Christ, I don't know," Jake says. He appears to regain his composure, brightens up.

"That was pretty killer though, right?" Jake asks the room.

"Oh, it was nuts!" Amy shouts, throwing her hands into the air.

"My God, having knees that actually worked again!" Melanie says, laughing. "And being able to run, and fuck, and all that. It was amazing."

"You two weren't weirded out having sex with men again were you?"

"I mean, we're both bi," Melanie says. "We just lean more toward the gay side of things. But no, it was cool. Blast from the past."

"I blasted you in the past," David says, and Amy can't stop herself, she whacks him hard in the crotch.

"Ah, my old-ass balls," David says, his face grimacing, he walks over to one of the VR chairs to sit down.

"Jake, honestly, are you okay?" Amy asks him. "You seem really bent out of shape right now."

"Oh, you ask him if he's okay…" David mutters, still grabbing his crotch over his pants, wincing.

"It was all so real," Jake says. "All the shit in the Bardo felt so fucking real. And now he's telling me none of that was programmed in."

"But the experience. Did it help you the way your therapist said it might?"

"Oh, right… that. I don't know. Maybe? I need some time to process everything. Especially with the fucking Buddhist bullshit."

"David, you had sex with the witch," Amy begins, is about to speak, then seems to rethink her approach. "How did that work?" She turns to the tech. "From what I gathered the witch and the zombie and all the other human characters were actors, correct?"

"Yes," the tech says. "They are in the rooms down the hall, actually. David is already familiar with the actress who played the witch."

"He's what?" Amy says, turning to Jake.

"Oh, did I not, uh… mention that…"

"You're fucking one of the actresses!"

"What? She's like my age for a change!" David says. "I can't wait for you all to meet her, she's a hoot."

"Well how does that work? You basically asked, what, if you could fuck inside the simulation?" Jake asks.

"Basically," David replies. "We are… uh… sort of dating…"

"David!" Amy says.

"What?! I knew you'd get weirded out if I brought it up!"

"Yeah, because we all talked about this ahead of time and how we were going to have sex, and I didn't know you'd be cheating, though why should I even be surprised."

"It's not like that. We're not dating anymore!"

"No, not—you, you idiot! That you would be cheating on *her!*" Amy shouts, exasperated.

"Oh, nah, like, it's fine. We're in, like, an open thing."

"Dave…" Jake begins.

"Oh what, it's the 2040s, and I'm fucking old as shit now. I could kick it anytime soon. So I'm going to ride my rocks off into the sunset."

"Very poetic," Melanie says, coughing.

"You all right?" Amy asks.

"Yeah, stupid Covid-30. I got the vaccine, so I'm fine. Just going to have a cough for a few days."

"Fucking Covid," David says.

The tech walks over to them. He waits for them to turn and focus on him.

"Would you like to meet the rest of the cast?"

…

The room looks very similar to the one they were in, this is what David thinks. The cast stand in a line, only 4 in this room.

"This is Brandon Bretterberg. He played the zombie slasher."

A tall man who looks to be in his 40s, shiny bald head, one of those vaguely albino type guys. Huge rippling muscles. Piercing blue eyes. Definitely intimidating.

"Sorry I killed you all," Brandon says, laughing. The rest laugh too, along with David, who can't help but think *dang glad he was just acting.*

"This is Maggie Hexum," the tech says.

A woman who looks to be in her early 60s, short bob haircut with tattoos on her neck and arms. She winks at David, who blushes.

"Is your last name really Hexum?" Melanie asks.

"Fuckin' A, right," Maggie says.

"And these two gentlemen played the police officers," the tech says.

"The who?"

"We didn't meet them when they were alive," Melanie says.

"Oh, you didn't? We must have flubbed the timing on their deaths a bit. In any case, this is Darvey Spilinger, and his brother, Clarence."

"How do you do," Clarence says, the younger of the two brothers. "Yo," the older of the two says, David catching him staring at his crotch and shooting him a look. Darvey seems to take the hint.

"The teenagers are in another room, if you care to talk to them," the tech says.

"I mean, we'll see them at dinner, right?"

"Yes, of course," the tech says.

"Then let's wait. By the way, when is dinner? I'm starving," Melanie says.

"We figured we'd let you all go back to the rooms on the compound, shower, dress, then come back in an hour. Sound good to everyone?" the tech asks them.

"Sounds good to me," Jake says, "I'm sure we all smell rank as hell."

The tech merely nods, David realizes not everyone is like him and will just say whatever the fuck they are thinking. And this is likely a good thing for the world at large, he can accept that fact.

"My fucking balls still hurt," David says, apropos of nothing.

Amy walks up and makes to hit him in the balls again, and David cries out, blocking his crotch with his hands. Amy starts laughing, then starts coughing.

"Oh, god damn it, Melanie, you gave me fucking Covid!"

Now David is laughing, he can't help himself. He's distracted, which is his downfall. Melanie walks up and knees him as hard as she can in the balls. David makes a sort of shocked exclamational noise that sounds something like "ouha," and then collapses to the ground.

"I should have stayed dead," he says quietly through gritted teeth.

...

Melanie feels great getting to shower and change into fresh clothes. Jake was right, she did smell rank as hell, but it was also nice to get to walk around, get the feeling back into the legs of her muscles. The adjustment is proving a little tricky. Yes, it was VR, but going from your 20s to your 60s in a matter of minutes is a really odd occurrence.

The dining area of the VR Experience headquarters is nice, a lot of sterile white, but the décor is comfortable. The facility is located in Western Massachusetts, in the middle of the woods and mountains, and it's very pretty. Melanie loves the view out of the floor to ceiling glass windows, with the sun just starting to set, and the pink and purple sky. The sight fills her with hope. The promise of another day to come, perhaps a decent amount of good years left in her autumn years to live and experience and soak everything up she can before her time is up.

Melanie had a cancer scare a few years back. Throat cancer. They managed to get to it in time, but the memory of the diagnosis, the feelings she felt thinking her time would be over soon, they stay with her. It's not something you really ever forget.

Except for in moments like this. In moments like this Melanie thinks maybe, just maybe things will be okay. Perhaps death will not be the end. And, even if death is the end, maybe when the time comes she'll have learned to accept her passing, and will go gracefully into that quiet night.

Melanie pushes the thoughts from her mind. Not today. Not now. She is here with her friends. She is here with her wife, Amy. Here with David and Jake, who they have kept up with over all these years.

This is her tribe. And so thinking, and smiling, Melanie sits at the large table to eat dinner and discuss the experience they just had with her friends.

"Oh my God, I'm so glad you shut off the pain receptors on our deaths!" Darvey says. "Can you imagine how bad it would have been otherwise, Clarence?"

"Hurt like crazy, I suspect."

"Hey, who played the old man?" Melanie asks.

"Over here!" a man about her age says, though this man is dapper, in a nice suit, no beard, close cropped grey hair and warm, friendly eyes. "I work at the college close by! But I heard about this and thought gee, this would be a real hoot to do, so I signed up."

"Well you did a great job," Melanie says. "Very menacing."

"Thank you," the old man, whose name Melanie has not yet learned, says. She does not bother to ask his name, and he goes back to his mashed potatoes and gravy anyway.

"So, how long does the film take to get made?" Jake asks the table at large.

An employee down at the end stands, and turns to face him.

"I'm in charge of cutting the movie together. It's quite a large amount of material, and then there's the matter of picking camera angles, and such. You'll get my cut together film, and a raw file of the entire experience emailed to all of you."

Now it's Jakes turn to stand.

"I want to, uh…"

The employee motions for everyone to quiet down.

"There's no good segue into this, so here we go. I have had a really hard life. I know that sounds lame to say, but that's the truth. After this trip to Lake George, the real trip, I tried to kill myself with a bottle of Xanax, and a bottle of Jack Daniels. And I'd attempted to with pills and booze about a year before the trip."

He can see the tears welling up in Melanie's eyes. It makes sense. She was the one who found him and called the ambulance. Both times, actually.

"And for years I got very close to trying to kill myself again. I was a bad alcoholic for many, many years. But that woman right there," and now he points to Melanie. "She saved my life. And we might have broken up on that trip, but our bond has never been broken. Anyway, to the point. A good therapist said that to finally get over my past trauma I needed to recontextualize it. To live through it again. To face it head on. And then Amy of course had the idea of trying this VR thing, and doing a horror movie experience. And we got to pick the setting, so that was when I asked you all if you'd be willing to go back. And David I believe your exact words were—"

"Heck yeah, get my young man dick back!" David yells, and the table bursts out into laughter, save for a few of the teenage girls, who very justifiably roll their eyes.

"Anyway, as you all can probably guess, it was a very unorthodox situation. Not the least of which because of the… um… sex."

"L-o-l," Amy says, covering her eyes with her hand, blushing.

"But I just…" and now the tears are in Jake's eyes, and he swallows down the lump in his throat. He coughs, clears his throat.

"I just wanted to thank everyone who made this possible. It was definitely really weird, but I do think it helped me get a sense of closure, despite it all being like a weird damn cartoon nightmare."

"Oh, Jake," Amy says. "You're one of my best friends. You're friends with all of us. It was no trouble at all."

"Yeah, motherfucker, you're stuck with us for a few more years yet, you swinging dick king of dudes," David says.

"I still hate you," Jake says, and smiles. David gives him the finger.

He locks eyes with Melanie. They don't have to share any words. They know each other.

The teenage boys are laughing, staring over at Maggie where she glares at them, sipping from hot tea.

"I saw you naked," one of them says, and the rest burst into teenage giggling.

"I can find out where you live," Maggie says, completely straight-faced, eyes never blinking.

The boys stop laughing. It's the teenage girls turns to start laughing, albeit a bit quieter.

"Hey one question, Mr. VR Experience man over there, what's your name?" David asks.

"Todd."

"So Todd, if the pain receptors were shut off on the deaths, how come when the witch, sorry, when Maggie," he points over at Maggie, who tips her steaming mug "how come when she wailed me in the nuts, like, how come I felt it?"

"You did?" the tech asks.

"Yeah, my balls are still sore, dude. And this was like, before Amy sack whacked me and Mel kneed me."

"More than what you deserve, you silly bastard," Amy says, taking a bite off a chicken tender. Melanie can tell Amy is actually a bit annoyed, and she doesn't blame her. David did cheat on her a bunch, and she just got to remember all of that crap in basically real time, closer to when the actual cheating occurred. *I'm so glad I'm not dating a man anymore,* Melanie thinks, staring at David, whose natural facial expression is more or less always overly exaggerated.

"Oh. Must be a programming error. Thank you for bringing it to my attention. I'm terribly sorry."

The tech looks nervous. Melanie doesn't blame him. The "pain blanket," they all had programmed into their characters (this was the company's term) was basically the only reason any sane person would volunteer to do something like this. The pain blanket kept all the pain from being too severe, and the pain was entirely shut off upon their deaths. So, any issue with the pain blanket programming, or whatever the techs referred to it as was definitely super messed up.

"Yeah, thanks for letting me get wailed in the stones without a pain blanket, you tool."

"David, just calm down," Amy says.

"You calm down! No one kicked you in the ovaries. And thanks for hitting me again, thank you *so much* for that. I feel like crap now."

Amy sighs. "They said they were sorry."

"So, Maggie," Amy says, turning to stare at the older woman. Maggie stops eating a burger to stare at her addressee.

Sort of stone-faced, ain't she? Melanie thinks.

"When did you and David meet?" Amy asks Maggie.

"Last week," Maggie replies, taking another bite of the burger, chewing for a very long time.

"Well, that was quick," Amy says. "And you're already fucking him?"

"Oh, more than that, sugar, we're living together."

"What the fuck, David?!" Amy yells at him.

"Look, we hit it off. Who gives a shit. It's the 2040s! Fucking live a little."

Melanie smiles, staring at all her friends. Looking at all these new people, all laughing, talking, eating together. She looks over at Jake, who gives her a nod. They've come out the other side of the VR trip, a similar yet very different trip to the one they actually took all those years ago. And Jake, there's this glimmer in his eyes, this is how it seems to Melanie.

And she does love to see Jake happy. That has never changed.

The house is huge, right next to Lake George. Jake feels silly because even all those years ago he never pieced together that the town name was the same as the lake name.

"Holy shit, Jake," Amy says.

"I thought you might like it," he says, to all of them.

They sit in the backyard of the house he's bought. Or, to be more accurate, the house he had built. It's been a crazy year, and no one realizes this more than Jake. On a whim a month after the VR experience Jake found a guitarist and drummer at an open mic night, and asked them to record a song with him. He still doesn't think he's much of a singer. He wrote a song about his time in the Bardo. For fun Jake posted the song online. Because why the hell not.

He didn't expect anyone to listen to the song. He really didn't.

To date the song has been downloaded 8 trillion times.

"I can't believe there's still trees and a lake out here," Melanie says. "After all the climate stuff."

"You can thank the children," Jake says. "Conservation efforts began in 2027. The area became protected wildlife, and tons of people planted new growth."

"Jake, this is…" Melanie begins.

"Yeah?" he says, then sips from a can of cola.

"Absolutely, dude, this place is nuts," David says.

"I had the money," Jake says. "I figured fuck it, why not look into it. So I looked. And there was a house in my price range."

"The fuck even is that now?" David asks.

"Buddy, you wouldn't believe me if I told you," Jake says, laughing.

The backyard has a great view of the lake, dense wilderness behind the house. They're laughing, and reminiscing. Amy drinks a margarita, David enjoys a joint, and Melanie nurses a beer. Jake drinks his soda.

He quit drinking alcohol 5 years ago. Even drinking in VR was too much for him, but he had to recreate everything how it was. Besides, with VR it was only the mental experience, nothing physically occurred in his real body. And he feels good. Yeah, he has a lot of money now, but it's more than that. For the first time in a long time he feels content. He feels like maybe it's okay to be, just, well... who he is. And it's a nice way to spend his autumn years, with a new zest for life, millions of fans (he's still wrapping his head around that), and a new album on the way in a few months.

He's gone through a lot to get here. And now, in a weird way, it feels like maybe it was all *for* something. He still has deep regrets, and fears, and he still battles the sadness every once and a while. But he finally feels like maybe, just maybe, that's okay.

David is asking him something. He tunes back into the conversation, smiling in advance. It's bound to be something stupid.

Melanie laughs at Jake's expression.

"What did you just ask me?" Jake says.

"Would you have sex with a werewolf?"

"There's… what?"

"You know, a werewolf, grrr."

"No, dude, I know what a werewolf is. You mean like, fucking it as werewolf, or as a person?"

"No, as a werewolf."

"Oh, dude, what the fuck is wrong with you?"

"I think I might depending on the level of transformation," David says.

"I buy this beautiful house so he can ask me if I'd fuck a werewolf…"

Melanie spits out her beer.

"Oh, we got a party foul!" David yells.

"Oh shut up," Melanie says, giggling.

Melanie stares at the sky. The sun sets, bathing the lake in a warm orange glow. The orange warmth of the setting sun paints her friends as they smile, and laugh, and react in animated ways to each other. And she stares over at her wife, Amy. And Amy leans in and kisses her.

And Melanie remembers the first time they came to this lake, to stay at this place. She remembers when they first fell in love, when the two of them were finally able to express that love to each other.

Melanie sighs, contentedly, taking in the lake and the surrounding trees. Staring at the sky. She squeezes Amy's hand, and they stay like this.

"I love you guys," Melanie says.

"Fucking laaaame," David says.

"Oh my God, shut up," Melanie says.

She smiles. They made it. All of them.

They survived the Lake George zombie slasher.

"Hey, what happened to Maggie?" Melanie asks.

"Oh, her."

"David?" Melanie says.

David bursts out laughing.

"She stole all my stuff!" he yells, breaking down laughing, falling off his lawn chair.

"Wow, you suck," Jake says, shaking his head back and forth.

Melanie knows a lot of people don't get to have moments like this. She's grateful for everything.

Soon the stars blanket the night sky, and Jake gets a fire going in a circular grey brick pit.

"We survived," Melanie says to all of them. They respond, David with "hell yeah," Amy with "damn straight," and finally Jake with "we did."

Melanie lies back in her chair, and smiles, staring at the stars in an ocean of night.

Official Playlist

Soundgarden - Burden In My Hand

Foo Fighters - Good Grief

Sponge - Wax Ecstatic

Pearl Jam - Even Flow

Nirvana - Come As You Are

Bush - Straight, No Chaser

Soundgarden - Blow Up The Outside World

Pearl Jam - Why Go

Local H - Bound For The Floor

Alice In Chains - No Excuses

Stone Temple Pilots - Still Remains

Mad Season - River of Deceit

Soundgarden - Fresh Tendrils

Hole - Doll Parts

Spacehog - In the Meantime

Bush - Alien

Sean Mala Thompson grew up in New England, and currently lives in the high desert of New Mexico with his long-time partner. He is the author of the collection "Screaming Creatures," and the novel "TH3 D3M0N." He is also the owner and operator of Nictitating Books.

You can find him on Twitter @SpookySeanT, also on Threads, Bluesky, Instagram, and the other thousand socials.

Printed in Great Britain
by Amazon

33958785R00129